Qais Ghanem immigrated to Canada in 1970. He graduated in medicine from the University of Edinburgh. Specialty training in public health, pediatrics, and neurology took place at Queen's, McMaster, Michigan, Sanaa, and finally, Ottawa U. Dr. Qais Ghanem has remained Clinical Professor U of O, President Canadian Society of Clinical Neurophysiologists, and Director of Sleep/Neurophysiology Lab, Military, Ottawa, and Monfort H.

Author Of:
Three Mystery Novels in English:
Final Flight from Sanaa – 2011
Two Boys from Aden College – 2012
Forbidden Love in the Land of Sheba – 2014
Co-authored *My Arab Spring – My Canada* – 2012
Book of Arabic/Eng Poetry: *From Left to Right* – 2014
Arabic: *Smashwords e-book Hiwar Bidoon Khisam* – 2017

Awards:
– The Canadian Ethnic Media Award (CEMA) x2, 2009, 2010 – Radio Category – for "Five Races in a Family of Four", and "Three Women Friends: Jewish, Christian and Muslim"
– Ottawa Community Immigrant Services Organization (OCISO) 2010 Media Leadership Award
– The United Way Community Builder Award
– Yemeni Canadian Community Award 2012
– The Arab Canadian University Graduates Association 2013 award for poets and authors
– Queen Elizabeth Diamond Jubilee Medal 2013
– Short List: Arab Ambassadors Award for Volunteering 2013
– Top 25 Immigrants to Canada Medal 2014
– Order of Ottawa Medal 2014

Comments on Qais Ghanem's book The Four Arabs

This is a fascinating book. I could not put it down and finished it within 24 hours!

Four Arabs: an old Egyptian who is a professor in Edinburg; his banker niece in London; her gay Christian male friend who is a real estate agent; and a conservative cleric meet on several occasions in London. They have one thing in common: an intense interest in what's happening in the Middle East, with its failure to deal with modernity, its dysfunctional political systems, corrupt dictators, poor education and many inequities, not the least of which revolves around women's rights.

The author cleverly uses his characters to debate these issues. Apart from the cleric, who provides the conservative understanding of Islam, the others are equally cleverly used by the author to raise and discuss controversial issues on the nature of divinity, scripture, our origin and destiny, dogma, identity, sexual orientation, the absence of a free press in Middle Eastern countries, whether there are "chosen" peoples on earth, and many other topics.

Readers, especially those who originate in the Middle East, will find this book to be very provocative but also very interesting. It is bound to be read widely and will be seen as a mini-encyclopaedia, a veritable curriculum, and a great conversation starter!

I highly recommend it to all who want to understand the Middle East and its three monotheistic traditions. It is both hopeful, in that the characters express hope for change, for the way in which the religions, and especially Islam, will find peace with modernity; and gloomy, in that the people being discussed still cannot let go of their great historical achievements, haven't learned and are unlikely ever to learn how to use logic, and always fail to listen to each other, and so consensus among them is impossible! There are undoubtedly some minor exaggerations, but the writing is fluid, the momentum never wanes, and everything is all done so beautifully, with great dollops of heart-warming humour!

Professor Abdulla Daar, Toronto, Canada
Author of *Garment of Destiny*

Qais Ghanem's *Four Arabs* starts with four Arabs involved in a Cairo car crash involving a drunk Arab colonel killing an Arab woman from Britain, sending her Arab husband into a coma and leaving their Arab host traumatised by the tragedy, which otherwise would have been a wedding reception. In this beautifully woven story, one can feel the tragedy of the Arab world and its self-inflicted wounds, which most believe are pre-ordained by Allah as the destiny of the Arabs, a never-ending curse that began in 1258CE with the fall of Baghdad and continues today in the Arab vs. Arab schism best reflected in the crash of cars in Cairo that Dr. Ghanem chose to jolt the reader. The addition of a gay Arab man from Lebanon with a flair for flirting with women adds to the richness of the Arab identity, so sullied by those guided by a seventh-century god living just beyond Pluto.

Recovering from his coma, the widowed Egyptian returns to Britain where the reader will find him with the other three Arab characters – his niece Samia in London; Sam, the gay Christian Lebanese who is a real estate agent; and Abdul-Raheem, an Islamic cleric uprooted from Yemen.

These are the 'Four Arabs' who fill Qais Ghanem's book with their opinions and discussions on 'Democracy, Deity and Death', which is the sub-title of his book, but in essence, page after page, these four Arabs primarily discuss Islam as well as Sharia, the 8th-century laws, whose weight has become the burden of a billion Muslims today.

Every Muslim home should have a copy of *Four Arabs* and they will find in it a reflection of the discussions all of us have, in varying degrees. Dr. Ghanem has done us all a tremendous favour and a service in using fiction to lay bare the truth we are told never to utter in public lest the 'kufaar' find a chink in non-existent armour.

Aden used to be the intersection where the Arab met the Indian and where Hindi, Urdu and Arabic interlaced with English in a rare coming together of two great people. Today a son of Aden has opened the window to a land that once was.

Four Arabs will titillate the atheist as well as the mullah. For we Muslims are sons and daughters of Hallaj who supposedly challenged Allah and Ghazali who justified the beheading of Hallaj.

Tarek Fatah, Toronto, Canada
Author of *Chasing a Mirage: An Islamic State or a State of Islam*

Introduction

Since my retirement from the practice of medicine, I have regularly met, for coffee, with a small bunch of elderly like me: Arab men and occasionally a woman or two.

It goes without saying that the conversation turns into a debate about the chaotic state of the Arab world. There is total agreement that things need to change, but there is no agreement on how. And yet we continue to be friends! Inevitably, we blame the military and hereditary dictators for the abysmal status of the Middle East. But, as we got to trust each other, we found that everyone recognized that the reason, perhaps the main reason, is in fact religion, albeit as managed and used by Arab governments and their agents on the ground.

I was born in the British Colony of Aden, now part of chaotic Yemen, to a very highly educated family of two medical doctors and four Ph.Ds., including father. And yet, most of my siblings can recite the Quran by heart, and pray five times a day, preferably in the mosque, whereby they expect greater rewards in paradise.

My doubt about the hereafter was triggered as early as the age of twenty, at the faculty of medicine of the University of Edinburgh, while I was dissecting a human cadaver, trying to identify the brachial artery, the radial nerve, and the left ventricle of the heart. It was a weekly ritual, and as I continued my dissection with my Scottish student partner Donald Grant, I could see the cadaver slowly disappearing over several months.

I did ask myself how could that poor man reconstitute himself when his body was slowly but steadily vanishing, down the drain, literally. Later as a physician I saw many dead bodies, destined for burial or cremation, which only reinforced my doubt in the fanciful stories one reads in all holy books about resurrection.

I wanted to believe! It is much easier and far less frightening than to deny all the scriptures. After all, how can they all be wrong? Which brings me to this final thought.

My father used to repeat what Stuart Chase once said, "For those who believe, no proof is necessary. But for those who do not believe, no proof is possible!" What more can one say?

To the billions who struggle with the concept of what happens to them when they leave this world, how they should treat people of other faiths, and whether and why their own faiths may be no better than the faiths or beliefs of others, after all!

Qais Ghanem

Democracy, Deity and Death

A Discussion by Four Arabs

Austin Macauley Publishers™

LONDON • CAMBRIDGE • NEW YORK • SHARJAH

A CIP catalogue record for this title is available from the British Library.

ISBN 9781528915670 (Paperback)
ISBN 9781528961332 (ePub e-book)

www.austinmacauley.com

First Published (2019)
Austin Macauley Publishers Ltd
25 Canada Square
Canary Wharf
London
E14 5LQ

I must acknowledge the influence of other writers, more learned than me, who have tackled the subject of the hereafter with courage and tenacity. They broke new ground and made it easier, indeed less dangerous for those, like me, who came after them. Although I do not agree with everything they wrote, I certainly learnt from Salman Rushdie, Irshad Manji, and Ayan Hirsi. But it was mostly the writings of Tarek Fatah that I read and admired over several years. That is not surprising, because I got to know him personally and have exchanged ideas with him, given that we both live in Canada, only five hours apart by road.

I also want to acknowledge the support I received from two surgeons who critiqued my work without necessarily agreeing with my opinions. These are my school mate, Professor Abdulla Nasher in Ottawa and Professor Abdalla Daar from Toronto, who has just launched one of the most gripping auto-biographies I have read, namely *Garment of Destiny.*

Chapter 1
A Wedding in Cairo

The wedding party was both well-organized and well-attended. Saleh and his wife, Sawsan, were pleased they had made the decision to accept the invitation. They had travelled from Edinburgh to Cairo, not the easiest of journeys, because it was Hana, Sawsan's favourite niece, who was getting married. Hana was Sawsan's eldest niece, and in her opinion, the kindest and most respectful of her sister's children. Her fiancé was from an educated, middle-class family of similar status to their own, and a recent graduate of the Law Faculty at the American University in Cairo. Following the reception, as guests slowly drifted out of the Nile Ritz-Carlton's Ballroom, Sawsan's younger brother, Hamdi, caught up with them and offered to drive them back to their hotel. It was on his way home, but he would have offered anyway. After all, he hadn't seen his sister since she had moved to Edinburgh years before.

At the hotel car park, Hamdi pointed out his small, battered, dust-covered Corolla.

"Here it is – my very own Almahroosa!" Hamdi said.

They all chuckled. The name was a familiar one in Egypt, given by many to their old, run-down cars, as it meant 'the safe one' or 'the guarded one'.

Hamdi opened the front passenger door for Saleh and the rear door for his sister, but Saleh switched with his wife so that she and Hamdi could sit closer together to chat.

"I can hear you quite well from the back. And you can catch up better like this. You won't get another chance for a while as we fly back to Edinburgh tomorrow."

"Thank you, my love, for being so considerate," Sawsan said.

Sitting in the back, Saleh caught parts of the conversation not drowned out by the cacophonous noise from the streets. Even at that late hour, the city was chaotic and the traffic relentless. The complete disregard for regulations, and other motorists, caused endemic congestion, made even worse by the absence of the Cairo Traffic Police, who had gone home for the day, leaving the city's drivers to fend for themselves.

More often than not, Saleh would suck in his breath or grip the grab handle even more tightly as the car narrowly avoided yet another collision. Glancing at him in the rear-view mirror, Hamdi chuckled.

"You've been away too long, my friend!" he said.

Twenty minutes later, Hamdi said, "We're almost there. Two more intersections and then you'll be safe in bed!"

He stepped on the accelerator pedal as he neared the traffic lights of the first intersection. The traffic lights had just turned green, but tended to change quickly. But as they crossed the midpoint, a black Mercedes-Benz G Class hit the right side of the car, massively impacting the front passenger door. Brakes screeched in all directions followed by a momentary, eerie silence.

Sitting dazed at the steering wheel, Hamdi became aware of his sister's limp body pushing heavily against his right shoulder. Blood trickled from her mouth and her eyes were only partly open.

"*La ilaha illallah*. There is no god but Allah." Invoking the *Shahada*, the Islamic declaration of faith, Hamdi turned his head to check on Saleh. He was unconscious but otherwise unharmed.

People started to gather around the wreck of the two cars. A few minutes later, sirens were heard approaching the scene. Minutes later still, an ambulance arrived.

Hamdi panicked. Two of his closest relatives were possibly dead. It was unreal, and he wondered briefly if he was having a nightmare, but the shouting of people surrounding the cars soon made him realize the horrendous reality of the moment. Hamdi himself had severe pain in his right shoulder, but could still move his arm and hand.

The ambulance took Saleh, Sawsan and Hamdi to the As-Salam International Hospital. Sawsan was declared dead and her body was transferred to the morgue pending an examination by the forensic pathologist. Saleh was admitted in coma to the ICU, with suspected intracranial hemorrhage, although the brain scan suggested a serious concussion instead.

Regaining consciousness after three days, Saleh was told that Sawsan had already been buried in compliance with Egypt's laws and Islamic tradition. Several members of his family visited him, the most regular being Hamdi, perhaps out of guilt for his involvement in the accident.

The first time Hamdi visited, Saleh wept inconsolably. In spite of his scientific background, he could not accept that the woman he had passionately loved for so many decades had disappeared, so violently, from his life.

During other visits, he reminisced about their amazing relationship. He recalled how they met; he a professor of biology at Cairo University, she a student in his class. How keen she was. How smart. And how beautiful. She was only twenty-one, and he was double that age, still unmarried. She fell in love with him, and admitted it, showing her strength of character, despite living in a society where women did not do that sort of thing, at least in those days.

He tried to put her off, and thought he had succeeded, but then he regretted his decision. He worried that their age difference would discomfit her family, but it didn't, and when he asked for her hand in marriage, he remembered how pleased they had all been and how he had felt so much younger than his forty-plus years.

Their marriage was perfect, except in one respect. Saleh recalled Sawsan's unhappiness after she discovered that she was unable to have children. They went through infertility testing as a couple only to learn that she had a bicornuate divided uterus, which caused her to miscarry repeatedly.

But she accepted her fate with courage. They toyed with the idea of adoption, but decided against it. He would have been a grandfather by now. And Sawsan would have been the kindest grandmother in the world. He wept silently lest the other patients and hospital staff heard. Hamdi came to pick him up when he was discharged. Saleh had decided to return to Edinburgh directly, so Hamdi had already been to the hotel to collect his luggage. On the way there, the mood was somber.

"So what happened to the driver of the G Class?" Saleh asked.

"Nothing!"

"What? What do you mean? In spite of my head injury, I remember clearly that you were already in the middle of the intersection when he hit you!"

Hamdi sighed. "Professor, this is a lawless place. Egypt is a corrupt country. Those of us who live here know there is no justice."

"But what did the police say?"

"The police are part of the problem. This country is ruled by people in uniform, whether it's the police or the army. When we were driving from the wedding, did you not see that nearly every building had a picture of our military dictator?"

Saleh nodded.

Hamdi continued. "These people in uniform make all the crucial decisions in our lives. And they can because they control forty percent of Egypt's economy. They monitor the press and TV channels. They appoint the university professors. They appoint the judges. What I did find out was that the driver of the G Class was a senior colonel in the army."

"Was he drunk?"

"Probably. But he wasn't tested, of course. The police officers at the scene wouldn't have dared ask him to take a breath test. And then there is his version of what happened, i.e. that he was there first and that I was at fault. I'm actually a bit surprised that I haven't been charged... yet. "

"How could he have been there first? The front of his car hit the right side of yours! If he had been there first, you would have crashed into the left side of his car. And Sawsan would be alive."

Saleh's tears welled. He took a tissue from a box on the back seat and dried his eyes.

"What will you do now, Professor?"

"I don't feel like doing anything, to be honest. And yet I must."

"Why don't you stay here? You're Egyptian. I assume you still have your passport."

"Yes, I have a passport. But I don't belong here anymore. I've been away too long. And now, with Sawsan gone, I feel even less Egyptian. Anyway, our house is over there, and all our things... and memories. Even if I were to come back, I'd still need to return to Edinburgh to sort everything out. I don't even know where to start. Sawsan looked after the house for us. It's never occurred to me how much she did until now."

"Are you in touch with your niece, Samia, in London? Sawsan used to mention her sometimes."

"Not really. London is quite far away. I used to see her when I attended a few annual scientific meetings in London, but I don't attend anymore. Maybe I should move to London. It would be good to be close to family. She has a daughter, Tina, at university. Did Sawsan tell you Samia is divorced?"

"No, she didn't. What happened?"

"Well, she's a very independent, forceful woman, with a mind of her own. I guess her husband couldn't live with that. The last I heard was that she was quite happy being single, and really enjoying her job as a bank manager. Hmmm... maybe I will move. As I said, it would be good for me to have family around, especially at my age."

"At any age, I'm sure. I'm so used to having an extended family that I, for one, would find it difficult to be alone for even a few months."

"You might be right. I'll phone her when I get back to see what she thinks."

17

"You do that! And if ever I get the opportunity, I'll come to see you in England."

"I'd like that. And thank you for driving me to the airport."

"Don't mention it."

Saleh spent the rest of the journey looking out of the window at the teeming, vibrant city that had once been his home, realizing he was unlikely to return. So, when they arrived at the airport, the farewell was muted.

"Have a safe journey and please keep in touch."

"Thank you, Hamdi. I'll try." They hugged and parted.

Chapter 2
London

By the time Saleh phoned, Samia had already heard about the death of her aunt, and it was she who suggested that he move to London so he would be closer to family. Even though Samia was single again by choice, she still understood the negative implications of the loss of his spouse.

For Saleh, the loss was far more palpable, not only because it was so recent, but because it was difficult to adjust to it in his seventies. He became depressed. All his former joie de vivre disappeared. He neglected to eat, but found himself consuming much more wine, or beer on warm days. And when he did eat, his food consisted of the unhealthy microwave snacks available at his nearest corner store.

He longed to go out for a coffee, or a meal, with his beautiful Sawsan like before, but that was no longer possible. He took to brooding endlessly during the day, because he had even lost the ability to enjoy reading.

What was especially hurtful was the silence of his closest friends; the people with whom he and Sawsan used to meet socially no longer phoned. Yes, they did phone to express their condolences, but after that, there was just an awkward silence.

He wanted to trumpet his isolation to anyone who would listen, but he couldn't. As a biologist, he wanted to remind people that man was a social animal in need of constant contact with his fellow men and women, but he didn't.

And then, as time went by, his weeping became less frequent, and his insomnia less exhausting. And he began the

19

slow process of organizing his belongings and of selling his house.

He kept his photographs, his desk and a lot of his books, putting them into storage. He could not bring himself to part with them, especially the books and journals which contained his own research. He knew he was never going to read them again, but they were like his children, the ones he never had.

Samia offered him a bedroom in her house while he looked for a place of his own. She also spoke to Sam, a real-estate agent and one of her clients, about finding a flat for Saleh, preferably within walking distance of her own house.

Sam was Lebanese and a real joker. Whenever he came to the bank, there was endless teasing. He was tall, muscular and handsome, in a rough kind of way, and would flirt with any woman, especially her, whether they encouraged him or not. But Samia liked him, and did not mind his behaviour, especially after she found out that he was gay. She actually liked him more after that, and met him on occasion for coffee.

Chapter 3
A Man from Yemen

Abdul-Raheem Ahmad Al-Absi was born in Cardiff, Wales, the son of a Welsh barmaid and a Yemeni sailor who had settled in Cardiff after retiring from P&O, a British shipping company which carried goods and passengers between Sydney and Cardiff, with bunkering stops in Singapore, Aden and Suez.

He was the youngest of three children, but the only boy. He had done moderately well at school until reaching adolescence, when he and his classmates began sampling the pleasures of life available in a liberated, modern British society.

This behaviour was, in part, in opposition to his father whom he found was becoming increasingly pious with each passing year. What he didn't realize was that his father, seriously worried about his son, had taken the advice of his *Imam*, and decided to send the boy back to Yemen. In Yemen, the boy would learn proper Islamic behaviour, he would become fluent in Arabic, and learn the Quran by heart.

So, Abdul-Raheem was sent to Aden, that busy southern port of Yemen, to live with a paternal aunt and her elderly husband, a strict Muslim, who had no sons, but only four daughters, one of whom he thought would make a good wife for the boy.

Abdul-Raheem resented both the restrictions imposed upon him by Yemeni society, as well as the discipline imposed by his aunt's husband. But he had to follow the rules, and so he directed all his pent-up frustration into his studies, regularly visiting the mosque and becoming firm friends with the *Imam*.

He quickly garnered a reputation amongst the local boys as a fountain of knowledge about all things Western. His upbringing in Cardiff as well as his fluency in English made them look up to him for guidance about faith and cultural conflicts, questions that abound at that age.

He began leading discussion groups at the mosque, and sometimes leading the prayers, and delivering the traditional Friday sermon, when the *Imam* was out of town or ill. So, despite his earlier exposure to western culture, he found himself in a position of authority, counselling the young men around him to follow the example of the Prophet Muhammad, and unreservedly to obey *Sharia* law.

Years later, political upheaval seized Aden. The socialist system which took over made his position in society precarious, and his advice undesirable to the new government.

By then, Abdul-Raheem was married with four children, and naturally considered his duty as a father to outweigh that to his flock at the mosque. And for the first time in many years, he thought about returning to Cardiff. But both his parents had long since passed away, and he had not kept in touch with his sisters, who were presumably married and living under the new names of their British husbands. And so, he also considered London, where he might find employment more easily.

"What do you think about moving to Britain?" Abdul-Raheem asked his wife, Fatima.

"It is up to you. You're the man of this family," she responded.

"Yes, I know, but I am asking you because you'll face a completely different society there which you may not like – or might even hate."

"Well, you were born there, and you grew up there, and you're a good man, so it can't be all that bad, I suppose."

"No, it isn't bad, but you'll feel the difference more than anyone else in the family. I was born there, as you said, and the children will soon fit in. They're innocent and open minded, and they'll absorb the culture around them. But do you want this for your children?"

"Do you?"

"I think it will be good for their education and their future. But they may lose their religion in the process, which I'd hate to see. Western society is falling apart because it has abandoned its religion, and with that, its moral values."

"In what way?"

"Well, your son might tell you to mind your own business when you advise him on something. Or he might not greet you when he comes into a room. Or he might disobey you and leave the house when you tell him not to."

"They do that already!"

"And your daughters will do the same, if you stop them from going out to meet their boyfriends."

"You're their father; it's your job to stop them before they bring shame and scandal upon our family."

"Over there, neither the mother nor the father can do that. The children could take us to court for forcible confinement."

"What's that?"

"It's what the lawyers call it when the parents physically prevent the child from going out. But if you are prepared to accept laws like these, we can go. My passport is still valid, and I can get passports for all of you. But you have to be part of this decision."

"You know best, I'll follow whatever you decide."

"Isn't it funny? The world accuses Muslim men of oppressing their wives. Yet when I ask you to make the decision, you kick the ball back to me!"

Fatima laughed. "There's just one thing I want to know; can you take a second wife – a white woman – in Cardiff?"

"Not unless we're divorced first."

"In that case, let's go!"

Abdul-Raheem could not stop laughing. He knew very well that he could have made the decision all by himself. With the green light from Fatima, however, he was able to move more freely and with enthusiasm.

He got in touch with two Yemeni friends, one in London, the other still living in Cardiff. He had erratic access to email, so he wrote letters instead, following up with a phone call to the one who replied first.

He also got the address of another mutual friend who lived close to Heathrow Airport, and who promised to put him in contact with a real estate agent friend of his. True to his word he did, and even offered to pay a deposit to the agent to secure the flat once it had been found.

Although there was upheaval in Yemen, there was no military conflict, so Abdul-Raheem obtained exit visas for himself and his family with a not unreasonable number of visits to government offices, and an equally tolerable number of bribes. And it was worth every penny to hear the excitement of his children as the plane began its descent into Heathrow.

Chapter 4
A First Meeting for Coffee

Saleh settled in with Samia and her charming daughter, Tina. He had been worried that they might find him old or annoying, but his fears proved groundless. Instead, he was welcomed into the family as though he had always been a part of it.

Conversations with Tina were especially fascinating, given the half-century difference in their ages, and Saleh learnt so much about modern life in a very short space of time.

A week after his arrival, Samia invited him along to her meeting with Sam at a café on Edgware road. She figured her uncle might want to mix with people from the Middle East from time to time, and maybe even brush up on his Arabic. Sam was also going to help Saleh look for his own place, although there was no rush.

Sam was already there, a fairly surprising occurrence given his notoriety for being late. But she'd got used to it by now, putting his usual lack of punctuality down to a cultural trademark.

She introduced the two men, and was happy to see that they got along immediately. But that also was fairly common in the East, where people who have never met, connect easily, talking for hours. Middle East politics was responsible for that because, regardless of political affiliation, the politicians' names were recognizable together with their widespread reputations for corruption. And while Middle Eastern dialects differed significantly, Arabs have classical Arabic, the language of the Quran, in common.

"Welcome to London, Professor. You may find it overwhelming and busy, after Edinburgh, but it's also a very pleasant place to live. It has everything and anything you desire. I'm sure you'll like it, and will never want to live anywhere else. I wouldn't. And I have no doubt that Samia is treating her uncle well. She is unkind only to me!"

He flashed a big smile at Samia, who grinned back. "Did I not warn you what a joker he is, Uncle?"

"Indeed!" Saleh said. "But it's obvious that it's kindly meant. So where in Lebanon are you from, Sam?"

"We're from Zahle."

"Ah, the famous river!"

"Yes, small but pretty."

"And where did you study? AUB?"

"No, at the Lebanese University. I wasn't clever enough for the AUB, apparently."

"What subject?"

"Business Administration."

"That's just what you need these days to make money. You don't get rich with a PhD in Biology. That I can tell you from experience!"

"But I wish I had been a doctor of something, doing research and writing books. That would have been fun."

"Samia mentioned that you run a real estate agency. Who owns it?"

"I do. Well, not quite; my partner and I own it."

"Well, there you are. You've just proved my point."

"Are you looking for a flat, Professor? Samia thought you might be – later on, I mean."

"Yes, I am. Somewhere within walking distance from here would be good."

"I'll keep my eyes open. Let me know when you get fed up with this lady here!" he chuckled while Samia feigned anger.

"Is your partner also from Lebanon?"

"No, Boris is Russian, actually."

"Really? How did you become partners? Where did you meet?"

"We met at a bar… a gay bar. Later, he joined my agency. I hope you're not shocked, Professor. Being Egyptian, I mean, and a Muslim… I imagine."

"Not at all. It's very common these days. It has probably always been common. People are just more open about it now. The stigma has gone, at least in the West."

"Do people still get their heads cut off, for being gay, in Egypt?"

Looking surprised, Saleh said, "In Egypt? No! I don't remember there ever being such a punishment there. Now, if you're talking about Saudi Arabia, maybe! I don't really know. But I imagine most people have moved on."

"Try selling that to our brethren in the Middle East."

"Yes, I am aware that we are light years behind the West, or 'the educated world'," said Saleh, making quotation marks with his fingers. "But most Middle Eastern countries have easy access to the internet, and there's a lot of information available now. When I was teaching, I read a paper by Bruce Bagemihl, who showed that the animal kingdom exhibits much greater sexual diversity than the scientific community, and society at large, have previously been willing to accept or admit."

"So, I'm not so queer after all?" Sam said, laughing.

"Not to me, my friend. But, to change the subject, are there many Russians in London?"

Samia joined the conversation, "I'm glad you changed the subject! In any case, we have to make a move. Tina's making dinner and she's asked me to get onions on the way home."

Sam smirked at her before replying to Saleh. "Yes, loads of Russians, but also many other nationalities. London's a melting pot. But I'll fill you in next time. We should make this a regular meeting. What do you think?"

"Brilliant idea," said Samia and Saleh in unison.

"Great! I'll call you."

Chapter 5
The Second Meeting

A month later, Samia and Saleh went back to the coffee shop on Edgware Road. It was a Friday, just after work, and the street was a hive of activity. Cars, buses and trucks idling while they waited for the traffic lights to change, and people walking, heads down, towards Marble Arch tube station, to start their journeys home.

They were already seated and had ordered their drinks when Sam arrived with another man.

"*Assalamu alaikum*. How are you?" he said as he approached their table.

Saleh responded warmly, "*Wa alaikum assalam*. It's good to see you again."

"I have a surprise for you!" Sam said.

"You're always full of surprises!" Samia laughed.

"This is Abdul-Raheem. He's from Yemen, of all places."

"*Ahlan wa sahlan*! Welcome. Please, take a seat."

"Yemen? Really?" asked Samia. "I've met a lot of different nationalities because of my job, but I don't recall meeting anyone from Yemen."

"Well, now you have," Sam replied, "and it just so happens that he needs to open an account as he's just arrived." Nudging Abdul-Raheem with his elbow, he said, "You need somewhere to put your millions, don't you?"

Abdul-Raheem looked surprised at first, but then realized Sam was joking.

"By the way, Samia, I do expect a commission!"

"You'll be lucky if I get you coffee after that remark!" Samia replied, but then relented. "What are you having? The usual? What about you, Abdul-Raheem?"

"Do they have tea? I'd prefer tea. But, I'll get them."

"No, no. This is your first time here. I'm buying."

Samia went to the counter to order, returning shortly with their drinks. "There you go. Tea for you, Abdul-Raheem. And this cup is your commission, Sam! So where did you two meet, anyway?"

"Abdul-Raheem's renting from me," Sam replied. "A friend connected us, and I found him a place to rent. He's moved with his whole family."

"Moved back," countered Abdul-Raheem. "I was actually born in Cardiff."

The three others looked surprised.

"We should have guessed," Samia said. "You don't have an accent. But you don't quite sound Welsh, either."

"So, tell us your story. Why have you come back?" Saleh asked.

"Things are bad in Yemen at the moment – and they're getting worse. So, I decided to come back for the safety of my family, and so my kids can get a decent education. Even my wife was keen to move, and she's never been out of Yemen. I guess that tells you what the situation's really like."

"How many children do you have?" Samia asked.

"Praise be to Allah! I have four boys," said Abdul-Raheem with obvious pride. "Muhammad, Abubakr, Omar and Othman. Om Muhammad, my wife, bore me one son every year…"

"But where is Ali?" Sam asked, pointing out that Prophet Muhammad had four disciples, the fourth being Ali.

"We also have two daughters," added Abdul-Raheem.

"Well, if we can help in any way, please let us know," said Samia. "I look after the Edgeware Road branch of my bank, if you really do need to open an account."

"Thank you."

"So how are you finding it? Being back, I mean," Saleh asked.

"Different!" Abdul-Raheem conceded. "But for access to information and news, wonderful! I had quite forgotten what it's like to read a real paper or to listen to real news as opposed to the propaganda fed to us in Yemen about the president."

"Indeed," Sam agreed. "But you may find that there is too much information, more often than not about something terrible that has happened in the Middle East."

"I agree. It would be good for one week – just one – to go by without something negative happening."

"That won't happen. I just can't imagine how things can get better in my lifetime. But maybe in our children's."

"And Yemen will be the very last country to improve. At least, in the case of Lebanon, you have some democracy," Abdul-Raheem said.

Sam looked skeptical. "I don't know about that. But there is a degree of power sharing among Catholics, Maronites, the *Shia*, and the *Sunnis*. But democracy won't come banging on the door. The dictators won't allow it. Anyway, that isn't Lebanon's main issue as I see it. It is rather that the state suffers permanent paralysis because there are so many religions and political parties. There have been times when the country had no president because no one could agree on whom to elect!"

"So, how are we ever going to enjoy democracy and stability?"

"As the Egyptian poet, Ahmad Shawqi, said, 'only with blood'," Sam said.

"We have shed enough blood, my friend. Why can't we find a peaceful way of doing this – just once?" Abdul-Raheem asked.

"They start off peacefully enough; think about the individual Arab Spring movements in Tunisia, Egypt, Syria and Yemen. But then the governments got involved and they all turned violent. The demonstrators were labelled 'terrorists' with the result that the leaders of the countries in question were able to incarcerate – even kill – them with impunity. Not to say that the same doesn't happen in the West; labelling someone a terrorist is the perfect way of getting rid of him," Saleh said.

"No, in Yemen it was even worse. When the students set up camp in Liberation Square, the president sent his marksmen to the roofs of the surrounding buildings to shoot them down." Abdul-Raheem volunteered.

"What? Openly?" Sam asked.

"Oh, no! The marksmen weren't in uniform! They were in plain clothes so that the president could claim the shooters were other students or civilians. Not only that, he sent his foreign minister, and other envoys, to the major capitals of the world to sell that false story to the presidents of China, Russia, and many other western democracies."

"Surely, they didn't believe him, did they?"

"I don't know. But they might have pretended to believe him – out of diplomacy."

Abdul-Raheem's mobile rang. He looked at the number, and after a brief conversation with the caller, hung up.

"Sorry, I need to go home. But we'll meet next week, I hope? Do you meet regularly? Here?"

"We haven't been," replied Sam, "But it's a good idea. Shall we?"

Saleh and Samia nodded their heads in agreement.

"Great! See you all next week, then!"

Chapter 6
Tribalism and Sharia

Just over a week later, Abdul-Raheem did take up Samia's offer for help and went back to Edgware Road to open an account. She saw him standing in the queue from her office and went over.

"Nice to see you again, Abdul-Raheem. So, you've come to open an account, I take it. Come with me; I can help you in my office."

"Thank you, Samia. It's nice to see you again, too."

Abdul-Raheem had all the paperwork necessary, so it was a fairly quick process. Once his account was open, they chatted for a while before Samia said she had to get back to work.

"But we'll see you next week at the meeting, won't we? Are you able to come?"

"Absolutely, I wouldn't miss it! Sam's already been in touch."

Back at the café the following week, Abdul-Raheem brought up the conversation they'd had about the Arab Spring movements.

"I thought a lot about what we discussed last week and came to the conclusion that the sacrifices made by the Arab youth were pointless. Nothing has actually changed. In fact, things are even worse now."

"Agreed," Sam said. "It's pretty depressing. But surely, we've learned something from that failure."

"Perhaps that dictatorship in the Middle East is the lesser of two evils," replied Abdul-Raheem, shaking his head sadly.

"But that's exactly what these dictators want you to think!" cried Sam. "How perfect would it be for them if the people never demanded their rights, and never dreamed of change, but were eternally grateful for the little they receive?"

"Well, I suppose it wasn't for nothing," conceded Abdul-Raheem. "We had peace for a while, and gained a few rights, Lebanon especially, because it is so progressive."

"Yes, but now Lebanon, too, has its fair share of murder, revenge and dispersion," said Sam. "Today, tribalism, racism and sectarianism are alive and well, under the supervision of police states, which encourage it."

"Yes, divide and rule, once again," interjected Saleh.

"Quite," agreed Sam. "In many cases, in the Middle East, a single tribe or sect controlled the government. Take Iraq, for example, where the *Sunnis* were in charge, until Saddam was killed, and the *Shiites* took over, decreeing that it was their turn. It will continue like that until people stop considering themselves only as part of a specific tribe, rather than thinking of themselves as equal citizens before the law of the land as well."

"You won't convince people to abandon their religion, their sect, or their tribe. That's ingrained in their psyche," argued Saleh, his voice rising slightly.

"No one expects them to abandon their faith or heritage, Saleh. But such allegiance should have nothing to do with their obligations as citizens. Think about the separation between church and state in Europe. That separation did not prevent Christians from celebrating Christmas, as it would not prevent Muslims from fasting the month of *Ramadhan*. As I see it, the other advantage would be that each group, big or small, would have equal opportunity for education, jobs, or election to parliament. It isn't easy, I know. But isn't it a lot easier than sectarian wars?"

After listening quietly to Sam and Saleh, Abdul-Raheem rejoined the conversation. Sam's opinion was too far removed from his own beliefs. "You know, *Sharia* is a comprehensive system of rules and regulations, ordained by Allah, and supplemented by the utterances of the Prophet (peace be upon him)," he said. "So, how can a man-made system replace it?"

Sam and Saleh paused, each of them recalling Abdul-Raheem's background as a cleric, before Sam said more gently, "And that's precisely the point. *Sharia* is fifteen centuries old. And while it was no doubt perfectly adequate when it came into being, society has become a lot more complex, and *Sharia* became outdated."

"The main problem is that *Sharia* is too rigid," Saleh added. "It doesn't allow for reform or change and this clashes with the changes that are happening in society. It has effectively become incompatible with modern society. The question is: How can this be resolved?"

"That's definitely a question for next time!" interjected Samia, "Otherwise we'll be here forever!"

"Quite true, Samia," agreed Abdul-Raheem. "I think we all have fairly strong opinions on the subject, but it's definitely worth discussing, another time. So, see you all here next week?"

"Did we not say we would meet at your place, Sam?" asked Saleh.

"Yes, that's right. I'll send directions, Abdul-Raheem. It'll be my honour and pleasure to receive all of you."

Chapter 7
At Sam's House

"Welcome!" Sam said, as he opened the door to his friends. Samia and Saleh had come on the tube together and had met Abdul-Raheem on the way.

Once again, it was a Friday evening, as this was most convenient for Samia and Sam who were still both working.

"Come in, sit down," said Sam, leading them through a hallway to the living room.

"It's a pleasure to have you here. I was starting to get a bit worried about going to that same café all the time. We've been, what? Three times, now, and each time we talk non-stop about the issues of Arabs and Muslims."

"And yet, still no solutions!" laughed Samia.

"My advice would be to heed the words of Saad Zaghloul, who said to his wife, 'It's no use, Safiyah!'" said Saleh, adding, "Even if it is slightly out of context."

"Slightly, Uncle?" exclaimed Samia, raising her eyebrows. "When he said, 'It's no use, Safiyah!', he meant that the medications she was giving him wouldn't postpone his death!"

Saleh smiled at his niece, acknowledging her correction.

"Did you hear that, Abdul-Raheem?" asked Sam. "Doctor Saleh says we should abandon these discussions."

"Don't believe him for a second! Anyone can see that he loves these discussions. As for me, I'll repeat what the Prophet Muhammad said, 'Even if they placed the sun in my right palm, and the moon in my left one, in order to persuade me to abandon my calling, I would never do that'."

"Yes," Sam agreed. "Wise people speak only when they have something useful to say, while the ignorant pontificate. Empty vessels make the loudest sound after all!"

Saleh added, "To tell the truth, I tend to avoid discussing politics, and especially with Arabs, because Arabs don't know how to conduct a polite or logical debate. I've found that they can talk, but that they don't know how to listen. I've found that the majority are convinced they already know the truth and are therefore unwilling to discuss the subject further."

"That's quite a generalization, Professor!" said Sam. "Is it really always like that?"

"No," Saleh said, acknowledging his second mistake of the evening. "Admittedly, even in Cairo, there was always room for debate at university lectures, while here in Europe, it is much more civilized. Europeans listen a lot more than they talk. And they don't interrupt or attack you personally, verbally – or physically! You can say what you like without fear of, quote unquote, disappearing, courtesy of the local dictator. In any case, the subject that interests me the most now is human rights."

"Don't worry, Professor!" said Abdul-Raheem. You're among friends. I'm a proud Muslim from Yemen, Sam is a Christian from Lebanon, and both of us are honoured to get to know you better each time, and to learn from you."

"Thank you," Saleh responded, "You've actually brought up an important point, in saying that, which is the misunderstanding people have about Arab and Muslim. A lot of people confuse the two, I think, or take the words to mean one and the same."

"That's very true, Saleh. A lot of people assume I am Muslim because I am an Arab from Lebanon."

"Yet you are only Arabic because you are from the Arabian Peninsula, and your mother tongue is Arabic. Your religion is not really part of that. While it's true that a lot of Muslims live in the Middle East, the majority of them don't – and also don't speak Arabic; the Bangladeshis, for example, or Pakistanis, Indonesians, Iranians and Turks."

Sam asked, "So what about your family, Saleh?"

"Oh, we are staunch Muslims! Some of my relations pray five times a day – and it has to be in the mosque, too, so that they get more points from God," replied Saleh, emphasizing the word 'points'.

"Well, at least getting up early gives a person a good head start on the day."

"Not so! After their dawn prayers, they go back to bed!"

Sam laughed, "I really envy people who can do that – return to sleep so easily, I mean."

"But why should they not?" countered Abdul-Raheem. "Having done his duty to Allah, a man would have a clear conscience, and therefore find it easy to go back to sleep."

"Clear conscience or not, many of these people are still guilty of sin, in my opinion!" said Saleh, "I recall a line of Arabic poetry that says 'Do not be fooled, for under that very tall turban, there is a hill of sin!' It reminds me of a video I watched on the internet about an Australian *Imam*, wearing a turban, criticizing the behaviour of other Muslims in Australia. He was condemning the idea of building more mosques, and of adopting *Sharia* law over Australian law, and supporting the idea that social functions should be held openly in community centers, rather than in mosques. He also stated that he knew of a few *Imams* who were polygamous and urged the Australian authorities to monitor their sources of funding. I was really surprised to hear that from an *Imam*."

"There are some bad apples, it's true," agreed Abdul-Raheem, "but why do we always focus on the wrong doings of Muslims? Why not also focus on the sins of the clergy in Australia and Canada against aboriginal children? You know, I read recently that the number of aborigines exterminated in North America was estimated to be nineteen million. Imagine! Nineteen million! That's more than the whole population of Syria... before the civil war, or the Netherlands."

"The number is shocking, I agree," said Saleh. "But, to give them credit, the West has begun a serious process of apology and compensation for the misdeeds of their clergy, who will no longer be able to continue the cover up."

"As a Christian, I'm aware of these atrocities, and that the church in Canada, tried to deny its responsibility," said Sam. "But Canada has an active human rights movement, which shamed the church into shouldering its responsibility. That's what's lacking in the Arab world. The problem there is that any criticism of the religious establishment is considered defiance of Islam itself. The Muslim ruler considers himself to be an extension of the rule of Muhammad, and his four disciples. But he forgets that they were distinguished, capable, and honest individuals. More importantly, he forgets that they lived fifteen centuries ago. Today, we need to be free to criticize whoever rules us."

Saleh responded, "Together with the bad apples, there are fortunately a few open-minded *Imams* here and there. I watched a clip of an Iraqi *Imam* the other day, speaking about this very subject. He was pretending to have a conversation with another *Imam* and said that people should question the authority of their religious leaders; 'governance is the prerogative of the people, not of God', he said, 'people should be free to rule themselves, as they see fit. And whoever claims that he has a divine right to rule, had better show me a written appointment letter from Allah!'"

"'Show me a written appointment letter!'" exclaimed Sam. "That's priceless! I like the message but have to say that it won't be so easy to question the *Imams* because they have the media on their side and use it to promote themselves."

"To be fair, even in the West, the media is owned by the rich. Isn't there a right-wing former Australian billionaire who owns so much of it that he can influence the results of democratic elections in the West?" Abdul-Raheem asked.

"Yes, but the Arab media is far more dangerous because it is often the only source of news for the local population. There's so much illiteracy that a much larger proportion of people receives its information exclusively from TV and radio. And, of course, from the *Imam's* speech at Friday prayers." Saleh observed.

"Shouldn't the same be said for Sunday sermons at church?" Sam questioned. "Admittedly, the lessons are probably more ethical in nature."

"The main difference is that attendance at church has dropped dramatically," said Saleh, "whereas that's not true about the mosque. And when education became universal in the West, people started to think for themselves. I suspect that this is partly why church attendance has dropped so much. In fact, some churches have been converted into mosques in order to accommodate the increasing Muslim populations in western cities."

"In all my years in Yemen, it's true that attendance at Friday prayers stayed constant," Abdul-Raheem agreed. "As for the messages from the media, it's also true that in a lot of cases, these are crafted to the advantage of the religious leaders and dictators."

"I've noticed that!" said Saleh. "Whenever I speak with a relative or a friend back in Egypt, I find that they have a somewhat different version of the news. You see, here, I always watch two or three different TV channels, to make sure I have a fairly reliable picture of what is happening in the world. But in Egypt, they don't, or can't do that, either because there aren't as many channels, or because there is so much censorship. Only last week, I watched an interview on TV. It featured a Saudi female professor, working in London, talking about her country. What she said could never have been broadcast on Saudi TV because she basically criticized the government. She said the Saudi government used Islam to promote itself, but forgot that Islam was a double-edged sword. She said that the government acquired legitimacy from Islam because the religious establishment allowed that. But that the religious establishment lost its own legitimacy as soon as it became beholden to the ruler."

"Saudi Arabia does have a reputation for being a fairly closed place," agreed Sam. "I have not been, but I understand that there isn't much leeway for free political thinking or discourse. As for individual rights of its citizens, these simply don't exist."

Abdul-Raheem interjected saying, "You both seem to be advocating against Islam, saying that it does not promote discussion and is therefore causing the deterioration of society. In fact, the Quran does the opposite: 'Read! Read in the name of your God, your creator' is just one example of that."

"I've heard this argument dozens of times," Saleh countered. "It's admirable that the Quran encourages reading, especially given that Muhammad himself was illiterate. But the Quran is replete with statements that contradict science as we know it today – fifteen centuries after Muhammad. And yet Muslims insist that Islam is valid and that the holy text is applicable to all time periods and to all places in the universe. If that were true, what does it mean when the Quran says that this earth will be inherited by the righteous?"

Abdul-Raheem protested, "My dear Professor, the interpretation of the Quran is an ongoing thing. Some *Imams* spend their lifetimes studying it."

"What has always fascinated me about the Quran, is how an illiterate man, like Muhammad, managed to remember every single verse he heard, and then to relate these back to Waraqah bin Nofal, who then managed to record on paper every word, without a single error. It's truly remarkable! I mean the Prophet himself said, 'I am a mere human, like the rest of you'. So why is no one allowed to say that maybe, I repeat, maybe, there is an error with a word or phrase?"

Abdul-Raheem protested, "You can say the same about the Bible."

"No, Abdul-Raheem, you can't," intervened Sam. "We Christians don't claim that the New Testament is the word of God. It is what the disciples recorded Jesus as saying and might not be word for word."

Saleh added, "And don't forget about the complexity of classical Arabic, the language of the Quran. Most people don't use it, preferring their own languages. And because of this, the Quran cannot be a transliteration."

Again, Abdul-Raheem protested, "But what about British English, American English, and Australian English?"

"No, my dear Abdul-Raheem, the language is practically the same, but you're talking about accents only and perhaps a few changes of words. The structure is the same. In the Middle East, each country has its own local language and dialect."

"And have you also thought about how complex the grammar of the Arabic language is?" Samia asked, joining the conversation.

"What do you mean?" Abdul-Raheem asked.

"Well, in English we'd use a single word to describe the action of a person regardless of who that person is. Take the word 'went', for example. In Arabic, it's different; the ending changes depending on whether we're talking about one man, one woman, two men, two women, or many men or many women. Six different forms!"

"I hear you, but I still love our beautiful language. It is the language of the *dhad*…"

"What of it?" Saleh interrupted. "Who cares if other nations can't pronounce that one letter? Can the Arabs pronounce the sound 'v' when they speak, like when they pronounce 'Venice' or 'Vienna' or 'Venezuela'? Or can they pronounce the umlaut of the Germans? Or that special 't' sound in the Hindi word *karta*? I'm sure that the Arabist scholars can pronounce the *dhad* as well as I can pronounce the letter 'v', because we made the effort. But I find this excessive pride in the language simply a compensation for the lack of significant, I mean internationally significant, achievements in the arts and sciences, where the Arabs have been left very far behind."

"I think you are being harsh on your own people, Professor," Abdul-Raheem protested. "All these Arab countries are just beginning to emerge from decades, if not centuries, of colonization. How can you expect them to compete? When they had their empire, it was the other way around, and it was they who spread knowledge and science."

Sam joined the debate. "I think what Saleh is saying is painful for us to hear, but we need to hear it, and we need to stop denying things. Otherwise nothing will change for the better. Educated people have a duty to say these things, not out of malice, but out of a desire to urge our nation to forget the past and to make sure that we are competitive in the future and can survive. And we have to start with the young, and with the subject of religion – not only Islam but Christianity, too."

"How's that going to lead to progress. You can't attack religion," Abdul-Raheem asked. "It will only create enemies."

Saleh countered, "But the divisions within the Middle East are based on religious and sectarian differences, and to a lesser extent, linguistic ones. And religion is the 'opium of nations', as we all know."

"Where does that come from?" Abdul-Raheem asked.

"From Marx, and the Bolshevik revolution," Saleh replied. "It spread because the oppressed and dispossessed were, at one point, waiting for divine power to help and save them from their misery. But it only happened when they eventually rose, fought and died for it."

"But the Arabs on the street look at their fractured nation, their weakness, their misery, their poverty, their poor health, their fragmentation, and fantasize about their golden past, which came on the heels of the Islamic conquests of Iraq, Syria, Egypt, the whole of North Africa, and even of Spain. How can you blame them?" Abdul-Raheem asked.

Sam answered, "We need to stop that, simply because such fantasy will achieve nothing today. Absolutely nothing! In fact, as the Professor said, it will be misused as a substitute for any possible attempt at recovery, through education, economic planning, democracy, healthcare, and gender equality. And the results will begin to show within one or two generations – that's half a century. But let's not forget that the world will have advanced even farther by then, and we'll be playing catch up for generations to come."

"But what I have said consistently is that we don't need to abandon our religion in order to do all that. How can prayers and fasting impede progress? They did not impede the golden days of the Islamic empire," countered Abdul-Raheem.

"I think that's where we differ. In my opinion, you can't have democracy if you also subscribe to the verse in the Quran that orders Muslims to 'obey God, the Prophet, and your leaders'. And you also can't have democracy if you continue to believe that a man can marry four wives and take concubines! Or if a female receives half as much as her brother on the death of their father. And, above all, if we don't have the right to modify or annul those laws of *Sharia* which we think are out of date."

Abdul-Raheem appeared upset. "But the laws of *Sharia* that you are talking about, have served us well in the past."

Saleh responded, "Served us well? Not at all. But even before we get into details, we need to agree that we should be able to change any and all laws that we think are no longer relevant to modern life."

"And who is going to have the right to change them?"

"By simple majority, in parliament."

"What parliament?" Sam asked sarcastically.

"Exactly, Sam. You've hit the nail on the head."

"But if that happened, what would be left of Islam?" asked Abdul Raheem.

"Would you accept me as a Muslim if I were a peaceful man who did no harm to any one?" Saleh asked.

"I would."

Saleh continued, "But I don't pray or fast during *Ramadan*, or perform Hajj in Mecca."

"That's between you and Allah."

"But that's the problem. If I don't, I will get into serious trouble."

Abdul-Raheem protested, "But nobody will force you to go to the mosque."

"In Saudi Arabia, the Mutawwa, that's the religious police, they would," Saleh said.

"That's an extreme case. Things will change there, too."

"OK, so why is it that I can't eat or drink in public during *Ramadan*?"

"Because you have to respect the feelings of others."

"So why don't they respect *my* choice *not* to fast?"

"Maybe they want to encourage you to fast."

"But I don't need their encouragement. I don't fast because I believe that fasting doesn't achieve anything except to help a few overweight people. And I'm not overweight. And here's another question: What about alcohol?"

Abdul-Raheem answered, "There are special bars for that."

Saleh asked, "But they are only for foreigners. Why the double standards? Why don't we follow the Quranic verse that says 'you have your religion and I have mine'?"

"Because such defiance might encourage the youth to do the same."

"But, in doing so, you're finding excuses to limit my own freedoms. When I drink alcohol, knowing that it might damage my liver, that's my choice. Why do you impose yours on me?"

"Western countries impose restrictions on drinking under a certain age, eighteen usually."

Saleh said, "On the basis of age of maturity, that's fine. In any case, the prohibition of alcohol by the Quran – the word of Allah – came in two stages. First the Quran said 'Oh believers, do not perform your prayers while you are drunk', implying that it was permitted to drink if one was not performing prayers. A later verse clearly prohibited wine, as it was called then. How come?"

Abdul-Raheem replied, "I don't see any need for alcohol. There are many negative consequences to drinking, from which the West is suffering today. Same with drugs."

Saleh said, "I agree totally. I hope that you will also agree that drinking is far more prevalent in the Muslim world than we pretend. Because of cost, it tends to be prevalent in the upper and middle classes. I have heard of leaders and actual rulers in the Arab world who have traded in alcohol, making millions. When will we, in the Muslim world, stop believing our own lies?"

"Don't believe everything you hear, my friend. So many people want to spread dirt about us."

Sam intervened, "Really? Listen, my friend! The Arabs don't need anyone to ruin their reputation. They are quite capable of doing that all by themselves. But we act like the ostrich, burying our heads in the sand. And why is it that the world does not spread dirt about the Indians, the Chinese, or any other nation?"

Abdul-Raheem looked puzzled. "Do I need to say it? It's because it's in the interest of our enemies."

Sam said, "There may be some truth in that. But the majority of Muslims are not Arab. The Pakistani father, who murders his daughter because she runs away to marry the man she loves, is not Arab. The Afghanis, who splash the faces of girls with sulphuric acid just because they want to go to school, are not Arab. And yet the Christian Arabs of Lebanon, Syria and Egypt are tarred by the same brush because we live among Muslims and use the same names."

Abdul-Raheem said, "I am ashamed of these actions committed in the name of Islam. It's a pity. The Quran addresses the Arabs with 'You were the best nation created in this world...' We must try to live up to that compliment from Allah."

"I heard that verse quoted many times throughout my younger years. I recall how proud I felt whenever I heard it. But as I matured and started to use my brain instead of my emotions, I began to question it, and to wonder why the God of all people would favor the Muslims, from among all the other nations that He created. Is that fair? If a mother bears seven children, is she allowed to favor the last one, to the exclusion of the other six?

"The official interpretation of that verse is apparently that some Muslims tried to persuade a Meccan Jew to convert to Islam. The Jew replied that his Judaism was better than Islam, so why would he contemplate conversion. It was only then that Allah conveyed that message to Muhammad in the cave of Hira, where Muhammad used to cloister himself regularly, to receive the verses of the Quran."

Saleh continued, "If we're to believe all this, then that implies that God must be extremely busy listening to the

45

millions of conversations of his seven billion humans who are capable of communicating with each other."

"Muslims believe that God is capable of all that. Anyway, it will soon be time for prayers, so I have to leave. See you next week."

"Thank God we've arrived at the end of this long discussion without anger or acrimony," admitted Sam.

"And without assassinations!" Saleh added.

Chapter 8
Edgware Road, One Week Later

At their last get together, the group had agreed to meet at their usual haunt on Edgware Road. Sam arrived first, closely followed by Samia and Saleh. It was the week before the fasting month of *Ramadan*. Although the group was small, it was diverse in terms of faith. Being Christian, Sam didn't practice *Ramadan*, and Samia had never seemed the type. He wasn't sure about her uncle, though.

As soon as Samia and Saleh joined him at his table, he asked them whether they wanted to keep meeting over the coming month.

"Let's ask Abdul-Raheem when he arrives," suggested Saleh. "He's the only one who's fasting, I imagine."

"I wouldn't mind continuing to meet. But, as you said, it depends on Abdul-Raheem," agreed Samia.

"Have you ever fasted, Doctor Saleh?" asked Sam.

"Yes, I used to when I was young and still living at home. My parents both fasted and they wanted me to as well, although they never forced the issue. It was actually convenient for them, because my mother would have had to cook for me, when she would otherwise have been sleeping or resting."

"You mean you were so helpless, you couldn't feed yourself?" said Sam with feigned outrage.

"As children we always understood that we had to stay out of the kitchen. That was my mother's domain. And she was proud of it."

"So, how did you find it? Fasting, I mean."

"It wasn't too difficult in itself. But it didn't work for me because my schedule did not change. I went to school, as always, but couldn't concentrate with an empty stomach. And when I got home, my parents would be sleeping, so I couldn't turn the radio on, or make any noise. When I left home to go to university, I didn't try fasting again."

Abdul-Raheem caught the end of the conversation as he joined them. "So why didn't you go back to fasting after your studies were over?" he asked.

"I saw no incentive to do so. I still don't."

"But, fasting during *Ramadan* is one of the cornerstones of Islam."

"I think the idea of fasting, in itself, is good – provided it reminds us that there are many starving people in the world. But that's not what happens in real life. What I've observed is that food consumption doubles both in quantity and quality during *Ramadan*. In some cases, it actually becomes obscene. I can't understand this need for sudden gluttony after a day's worth of fasting. Don't believers get their rewards in paradise?"

"I detect some sarcasm in your question, Doctor. I don't think that's appropriate," Abdul-Raheem responded.

"My apologies. I don't mean to offend anyone."

Sam intervened, breaking the tension. "But *Ramadan* isn't just about fasting, is it? What I understand is that people are also quite generous to those who have less than them during this time. But here's a question: How do people figure out who's poor and who isn't?"

Abdul-Raheem thought for a moment before replying. "I think it's possible to do this within small neighborhoods. Yes, some families are generous towards the poor, but that's a small minority who are really wealthy. In the Muslim world, the so-called middle class is really only just getting by."

"I've always felt that the poor should not be required to fast, because they're deprived, or relatively deprived, throughout the year in any case," said Saleh.

"I think that's a good point, Uncle," agreed Samia.

"But there can't be different *Sharia* rules for the poor. Poor Muslims are also required to fast," Abdul-Raheem said.

"Why not?" asked Saleh. "Wouldn't it make sense for really poor people to be exempt from fasting? I mean, if fasting is designed to remind the rich that the poor are starving, and that they should help them, then one could say that the poor fast all the time. Let's remember that fasting is also a duty in other religions, presumably for the same reason."

"Why shouldn't there be different rules for the rich and the poor?" questioned Samia. "The poor don't pay alms, or *zakat*, because they have no money, whereas those with money are supposed to give."

"I agree," said Saleh.

"As a Christian, who used to live in a predominantly Muslim community, I found it very inconvenient to go about my business during *Ramadan* because nobody got anything done," added Sam. "Let's be brutally honest here. Even at the best of times, Arab society functions with minimal efficiency. There are probably good reasons for that. But during the month of fasting, it gets even worse. If that's possible! And yet one can't protest. People just make excuses, saying that they can't function when they're hungry, thirsty or sleep deprived."

Abdul-Raheem interjected, "But it's the truth! Would you be able to work as effectively under those conditions? Doctor Saleh has already admitted that he couldn't!"

Sam protested, "But a whole month? I don't know of any other societies which abandon normal function for an entire month! And the worst part is that it's never at the same time of year, but about ten days earlier each year because the *Hijri* year is shorter than the western one."

"What about the Parisians who migrate to the French Riviera every August?" Saleh questioned, laughing. "Although, admittedly, they do leave a skeleton crew behind so that the city and services don't collapse!"

Sam agreed, "Yes, I'd forgotten about that! No nation is perfect, I suppose!"

"There is no perfect society, nation or religion. But the West always focuses on the faults of Islam," Abdul-Raheem said.

"That's a convenient thing to say," Saleh interjected. "But, on the contrary, I think our biggest problem is the near total lack of self-criticism. Without it, there is no improvement. And so Arab society continues to delude itself that it has wonderful traditions, culture, language and, of course, religion."

"But to get back to *Ramadhan*," said Abdul-Raheem gently, "I've fasted for many years, and find the month to be one of peace, tranquility and deep meditation. I actually look forward to it, although if I'm very honest, I'd also admit that I start looking forward to its end by the third week."

"Well, you're a lot stronger than any of us. A week would be more than enough for me! But I don't fast, and I have no spiritual attachment to *Ramadan*, so my observation is quite different to yours. I see people gorging themselves on two huge meals between sunset and sunrise to the extent that some actually gain weight!"

"I think there's some exaggeration in what you just said, but there it is. Let's agree to disagree," said Abdul-Raheem.

Saleh smiled his consent, adding, "I should perhaps qualify my statement by saying that this applies to the rich. The poor, as usual, have no choice."

"The Catholics also fast, during Lent, a period of forty days," said Sam. "It goes back to Moses who started this tradition when he retired to Mount Sinai. But at least we know that it will fall in either March or April. We need to invent a hybrid religion called Chrislam! What do you think?"

Saleh smiled broadly. "I don't know why there's all this confusion about the start of *Ramadan* anyway. Scientifically, it's possible to predict, years ahead, when the crescent of the moon will make its first appearance."

"Religious rituals can be beneficial sometimes – as reminders to people to behave in a certain manner, even if they don't influence my own! Life's too short! Why not just be good, caring people to our families, friends and neighbors?" Sam asked.

Saleh disagreed. "I personally don't find that praying five times does any good. There's one ritual which ought to change. There's a verse in the *Quran* that says prayers prevent wrongdoing and sexual sin. But I find no evidence of that from my own observations of those who pray regularly. In fact, before I left Egypt, I knew lots of those people."

"That isn't an acceptable statement, Doctor!" Abdul-Raheem retorted. "What evidence do you have that this is so?"

"Nothing specific, but I knew many men who prayed regularly, yet went about their daily lives oblivious to that verse. It was almost as though their prayers had simply become an automatic routine, rather than something to think about. It's the same with drinking alcohol, but at least that doesn't involve other people – unlike sex."

"But how do you know their sins wouldn't have been even more frequent if those men had stopped praying?" Abdul-Raheem asked.

"Well, of course I don't know that! I would need to conduct a controlled trial or experiment to answer that question."

Sam intervened, "I noticed, Professor, that you only mentioned men. What about women?"

Samia quickly intervened, "Excuse me! I'll have you know that women don't commit sins, or if they do, it's purely out of love or loyalty to men – who lead them astray!"

"What planet are you living on, Samia?" Sam asked her incredulously.

"I'd say you're definitely outnumbered, Samia," said her uncle. "But is there really any doubt in anybody's mind that ninety percent of all wrongdoing is committed by men? I'm quite convinced that if women were somehow able to biologically bear children without the need for men, our world would be a place of peace and tranquility!"

"A truer word has never been spoken, Uncle!"

Chapter 9
At Samia's House

After *Ramadan* and the celebrations of Eid-al-Fitr, the four friends met again, this time at Samia's house.

"So, did everyone enjoy the Eid, then?" Samia asked her guests.

Everyone nodded their heads, smiling.

"It was a good break, but it's nice to get back to our discussions," said Abdul-Raheem.

"It certainly is," Samia agreed.

"And isn't it fortunate that we all have such different backgrounds that make for such lively conversations?" Abdul-Raheem asked.

Sam agreed. "Quite different; a biology professor, a cleric, a banker, and myself, a real estate agent. Did you always want to be in finance, Samia?"

"Well, I was always good at numbers."

"I'll bet your father is proud of you," said Sam.

"My father died when I was little, but my mother is impressed. She's Uncle Saleh's youngest sister."

"For an Arab woman, I think yours is a great achievement," said Abdul-Raheem.

"For an Arab woman, who does not usually get the same opportunities, then, yes, perhaps it would be an achievement," agreed Samia. "But not for a British woman."

"They're ahead of us in such things," Abdul-Raheem concurred.

Samia smiled. "They're ahead in everything!"

"Hmmm… perhaps not in everything. We shouldn't ignore our own traditions and customs."

"Such as?"

"Such as being modest, exchanging greetings, respecting seniors… The Quran sets out a lot of good rules for social interaction. For example, it specifically tells us not to enter the homes of others without their permission, and to always greet people and show them respect."

"But people here don't enter the homes of others unless invited. And they do use greetings. But it's true that they don't use the exaggerated greetings, famous in the East, where everyone is either a brother or a professor."

"Where's the harm in calling people brothers?"

"I didn't say there was any harm; I just wanted to show that all the titles we heap on people, and all the bragging we do about how many cousins we have, is part of a tribalism that we cannot get rid of – the same tribalism that doesn't allow the Arabs to espouse democracy."

"But tribalism gives us a sense of personal security – because the state doesn't. If the state provided individual and collective security and human rights, as happens in the West, we wouldn't need tribalism."

"You're absolutely right. What we need to do is to establish equal rights for the rich and the poor, for men and women, for black and white, and for the healthy and the handicapped."

"And why shouldn't we brag? Especially about those of us who are achievers and innovators. Here in the West, they show off their artists, writers and thinkers – even their actresses!"

"Of course! I agree, but only if the evaluation is accurate, not exaggerated. I mean, we even brag about food! Can you believe that? For us in Egypt, it's *mulukhiyah*, while for you in Yemen it's *saltah*. They are two very ordinary dishes, but you'd think they were the equivalent of caviar! And as for people, I've heard that the Yemenis are quite convinced of their superior intelligence!"

"I've heard that too!" Sam interjected, laughing. "But the word 'intelligent' can also mean 'shrewd' or 'crafty'!"

Everyone laughed.

"So, how did you hear about our *saltah*?" Abdul-Raheem asked Samia.

"The same way you heard about our *mulukhiyah*. And the same way we both heard about fish and chips here in the UK."

"This talk is making me hungry!" joked Sam. "Shall we not change the subject? I'm actually surprised that Samia hasn't raised the issue of women's rights, yet, in any of our discussions. So, how about it, Samia?"

Samia looked over at Sam, slightly taken aback at the shift. "But it's a massive subject! Where do you want me to start?"

Sam smiled. "Wherever you like."

"But the audience is all male!"

"Well, here's your chance to convince and convert us!"

"A demanding task! Especially given that Arab men have been brainwashed since birth," replied Samia critically. "A lot of them probably think that a woman is born with half a brain! But why wouldn't they? I mean, her evidence given in *Sharia* court is worth half that of a man. And her inheritance, too, is only half of his. And she can be one of four wives. And she can't travel without a male guardian. And, in some countries, women can't drive or go swimming when men are in the pool. And don't even get me started on the pathetic belief some men have that a woman gets sexually aroused if she rides a bicycle or a horse!"

"Be fair, Samia," Abdul-Raheem intervened. "In the West, too, women were expected to ride side saddle. I once saw, many years ago, a movie clip of the Queen riding side-saddle during a Trooping the Color inspection. And what about the law that now allows Saudi women to drive? You have surely heard about that?"

"It's good news that the Kingdom is waking up at last. I'm not sure why there's a waiting period of nine months. It must be a mere coincidence that it's the length of a pregnancy! It's a good start, but there could be much more in the future. As for the Queen riding side-saddle, she only did that during Trooping the Color, out of respect for tradition. Women started riding astride in the early twentieth century! And who told the Arabs that women get sexually excited when they ride? Did anyone ask a woman about that? Let's say it's true. Who cares?"

Abdul-Raheem blushed, despite his brownish skin. "This is a rather delicate subject. Let's leave it at that."

Sam came to his rescue. "But let's not forget that the Crusaders, who left to wage war in the Middle East, were known to force their women to wear chastity belts."

"Yes, I did read that," Samia agreed. "But that was in the eleventh century – one thousand years ago! I can't wait one thousand years for change while continuing to listen to men who believe our place in society is in the kitchen – or the bedroom!"

"At least things are changing, Samia," countered Sam.

"Not fast enough. Take education, for example. I mean, it's the heart of the problem. We can't begin to discuss the sorry state of the Arab world without facing the horrific statistics about the status of women. Literacy rates are already abysmal for men, but they're around double that percentage for women. Did you know that, in Egypt, thirty five percent of women are illiterate? That's fifteen million women! In Israel, the percentage is only two. And it wouldn't surprise me if many of those were Palestinian. When it comes to the status of women in general, reports show that Yemen is at the bottom of the list, and that Saudi Arabia is close behind, even though its GDP is thirty times that of Yemen! I wish more people were able to read the wonderful poems of Hafez Ibrahim about the role of women."

"The latest figures I saw indicate a literacy rate of 80% among men, but only 40% among Yemeni women. It takes time for progress to occur," Abdul-Raheem said.

Saleh intervened, "Several years ago, I attended a scientific conference in Yemen. While I was there, I was invited to dinner by a senior military officer. His wife did not join us for the meal, so I asked after her. He raised his hand, as though to waft away an insect, and said that a woman was merely a vessel in which one sows one's seed and hopes that a plant would grow in it! I was so dumbfounded that I didn't know what to say. Later in the conversation, I mentioned the achievements of some of the women I had met over my career. But his response was: 'And what do we have to do with those infidels in Europe, my dear Professor?'"

"To be fair, it isn't only Islam that gives women that status," said Sam. "I've read in the Old Testament that, if there was no proof of a bride's virginity on her wedding night, she would be stoned to death by the men in the town. Thank God we've moved past such barbarism!"

"Yes," Samia said, "but, how can we move past that stage, if we're not even allowed to expose these horrendous customs, or discuss them freely, without being threatened?"

"There are some hopeful signs of change," Sam said. "I saw a TV interview on the Egypt Oxygen channel the other day. The interviewee was a young Egyptian woman, who had immigrated to Canada, but was in Egypt visiting family. It was clear that she was very patriotic, but it certainly didn't stop her from being honest about her country. I downloaded a transcript of the interview; it's here on my mobile; let me read it to you.

'*GPS doesn't work in Egypt. I went downtown and found Cairo like a graveyard, with filthy streets, and buildings in ruins. I was shocked by the standard of living here, and the increased use of hijab. Military rule shouldn't be allowed in the first place – in any country that respects its people. In Canada, there is gender equality at the highest level. In Egypt, they impose military law, using the excuse of fighting terrorism. Instead they use it to arrest the legitimate opposition. Why don't they want the country to have a legitimate opposition? Is the president sent from God? Does he not make mistakes sometimes? The ruler of the country is there to serve the people. All the ruler wants to hear is applause! And when a citizen tries to defend his country, he finds himself in jail. And emergency laws are there only to prevent the opposition from entering the election process*'."

After listening to Sam, Saleh said, "The biggest problem with the Arabs is that they deny their faults, and yet they lag behind the democratic world in everything. And anyone who dares to blame Islam for that lag immediately earns the label 'apostate'. And we all know what the punishment for that is!"

"But this is not the problem of Islam only," said Abdul-Raheem. "You'll find it in America, Europe, Japan and India. For example, no one dares to say that 9/11 was an inside job to plunder the wealth of Afghanistan and Iraq. If they did, they'd be lynched!"

"Not true," Sam said. "Dozens of highly qualified engineers, and aviation and combustion experts have said just that, and the internet is full of video clips documenting it."

"So, how come the Americans didn't buy into that?"

"Oh, I think thousands of Americans were convinced, even though they tend to have a superficial understanding of world politics. But the propaganda from the Bush administration, and from later administrations, has been relentless, and is backed by endless government money. The other problem, in my opinion, is that the Americans, as a nation, are naive or blind to the injustices in their country, just like the Arabs, and they think that their government is wise, even noble, and couldn't possibly commit such a heinous crime that would kill three thousand of their own citizens. After all, the USA is the leader of the free world. For many, it's simply unthinkable."

"'God is kind to a man who recognizes his own limitations'," interjected Saleh. "I am sure you are all familiar with this saying. And yet, regardless, the Arabs have an inflated opinion of themselves, their language and their religion. I remember growing up in Egypt hearing people referring to a stupid person as a *hindi*! And yet take a look at India today! The Indians were savagely ruled by *Maharajas*, and then by the British colonial empire, yet today the country is a respected nuclear power, and a functioning democracy."

"You can't compare the Arabs to the Indians," Abdul-Raheem protested. "India is a single country with one government and a population of over one billion Hindus, Muslims and Christians. The Arabs, on the other hand, belong to many countries each with each own government, most of which distrust each other."

"Yes," responded Saleh, "but the Arabs have a common language and a more or less common religion – excepting the division between *Sunnis* and *Shiites*, and the Christian minority, like Sam. The Indians have numerous languages and more religions, even if Hinduism is dominant. But while the *Sunnis* and *Shiites* hate each other, the Hindus live in peace with their Muslim minority. For the longest time, the president of India was a Muslim."

Samia jumped in. "The latest I heard is that India had banned '*talaq*', that ridiculous Islamic divorce law which enables a husband to immediately annul his marriage by saying '*you are divorced*' three times! Why can't the Arab Muslims do that, too?"

"It is a one-sided practice, I agree," Abdul-Raheem responded. "But we have to be fair, Samia. Think about the practice of *suttee*, where a woman would be expected to burn herself on her husband's funeral pyre. Even though it has been outlawed, today a widow goes from being called 'she' to being referred to as an 'it' after her husband dies. What could be more demeaning than that? That system is saying that her life is only valid while she belongs to a man!"

"That's a good point. But there's also real progress in Indian society, and their religion seems to allow it. I admit that I don't know much about it, but when I look at the progress made by Indian immigrant communities here in England and in other parts of the world, there's simply no comparison. How many MPs or city mayors of Arab origin are there?"

"I don't know. None that I can think of."

"Precisely; I rest my case. Although to be fair, I know plenty of Arabs in equally prestigious professions. Most came here because of lack of opportunity in their own countries, or because of political or religious persecution, especially after the military dictators took over."

"Military dictators have demonstrated that they're disastrous rulers," Sam declared. "They're so used to giving orders that must be obeyed. They don't understand democracy, where you give and take and have to compromise sometimes. They don't know how to listen."

"Agreed. But don't forget to include the Islamic government of Morsi in Egypt," Samia added. "It also failed. We need to make sure that people understand that only true democracy and pluralism will work in future. Religion should not form the basis of government – anywhere. Islam tell its followers to 'Obey *Allah*, and his Messenger, and those who are in charge of you'. That's *carte blanche* to all the dictators, sheikhs and kings to demand total obedience from their subjects. That might have been OK a thousand years ago, but it isn't today."

"That text should not be taken literally, Samia," Abdul-Raheem said. "Those in charge of you can also mean your parents who bring you up. And obedience of parents is something positive. Wouldn't you agree?"

"Yes," Samia replied, "There are already excellent verses from the Quran which deal with obedience to parents. Here we are so proud of our wonderful, precise Arabic language, and yet we cannot decide what the phrase '*ulil amri minkum*' means? In other words 'those who are in charge of you'. It can mean your parents, but can also mean your teacher, a policeman, the mayor, an *Imam*, the minister of education, but also the king, all his sons, nephews, cousins and…"

Saleh interrupted, "Look, my friends! Here we are, fifteen centuries after Muhammad, arguing about the nuances of text that belong to that era. What a waste of valuable time! We need to move on. Islam needs to move on before it becomes irrelevant to the millions of teenagers who will populate the world after we're gone. Islam served a great purpose when it arrived. But nothing can be perfect for every place, every era and every nation. I know some will label me *kafir* for saying this, but it's our duty to discuss these things, if nothing else, for the sake of our grandchildren. The world banned slavery and the Muslim world eventually followed suit. We need to do that with a lot of other 'laws' and 'customs'. There's still controversy about *hijab*, but I predict that it will virtually disappear within one more generation."

"But there should be no controversy. The verse about *hijab* was directed at the women in the Prophet's family," said Abdul-Raheem.

"No, it wasn't!" Samia retorted. "The verse says 'O Prophet, tell your wives and your daughters, and the wives of the believers to lower their robes.' The believers here can only mean *all* Muslims."

Abdul-Raheem said, "I'm most impressed with your knowledge of the Quran, considering that you don't…"

Samia butted in, "Don't believe in it? Whether I do or don't is irrelevant. I insist that we be accurate when we use it to support an argument. That's all. I cannot let some so-called scholar interpret it the way *he* wants. If you're going to use it to affect the lives of millions of marginalized women, like me, then I have a right to read it in my own language and to interpret it as I see fit. These so-called Islamic scholars don't have a monopoly on the Arabic language or its nuances."

"I agree," Saleh added, "especially because the issue of *hijab* or non-*hijab* has affected the status of Muslim women and how they are looked upon and treated in the West. When Muslim women were confined to their own countries, there was no controversy. But now millions of them call Europe and North America home, yet keep their customs. Surely, the Germans, Brits, Canadians and others have a right to know how these foreign customs will influence their own societies, especially with respect to their daughters. Imagine if millions of women went to Saudi Arabia and started walking around Riyadh in shorts. Don't you think the Saudis should have the right to evaluate how this might negatively affect Saudi culture and customs? I think they should, within reason."

"Lots of things need to change in Islamic societies," Samia said, "and those of us who call for change are actually the ones who care, especially where it concerns women's rights. It would be easier – and safer – not to care. But how can a person remain silent while men throw acid on girls' faces because they don't cover them? Or when a girl is murdered by her own family because she left the abusive husband they chose for her? It happened right here in the UK with the Kurdish girl, Benaz. Her father and uncle lured her back home, killed her and then buried her in a suitcase in their back garden!"

"Yes, that was sickening," Sam agreed, "and even more so because they both escaped justice by fleeing to Iraq."

"And what about that vicious custom of female circumcision?" Samia asked. "It's nothing more than barbaric clitoral mutilation that deprives women from reaching orgasm. What purpose does it serve? What I'd like to know is how the men in those communities would feel if someone amputated the heads of their organs at birth. Isn't that little organ what nature or God meant them to have? Why would they want to interfere with God's creation?"

There was silence from the three men, as they tried to imagine the situation in their own bodies.

Samia continued, "All this talk about it being hygienic is not true. And why are women considered unclean when they are menstruating, and therefore cannot pray or fast? If it was out of kindness and consideration, then why are they then supposed to perform the skipped rituals after their periods have ended?"

"This is obviously a subject you are passionate about, Samia," said Sam, "and I certainly will have a lot to think about now. But it hasn't always been a bed of roses for Western women. So how did they manage to gain their rights?"

Samia smiled faintly. "I apologize for monopolizing the conversation about women, but you're right, I do have strong opinions on this subject. As for Western women, believe it or not, there's a verse in the Quran that sums it up best: *Asu un takrahoo shay'an wa huwa khairon lakom*. It basically means 'from adversity comes good'. I think many of the rights were gained as a result of the World Wars. When the men left to fight, the women took over their positions in both offices and factories. They suddenly found themselves as important as men, and they also mixed freely with the men who remained.

It also came at a time when women were catching up with men in education, and when the influence of the church became less important in everyday life."

Saleh interjected, "If that's the case, Samia, there's a major hurdle. The religious principles of *Sharia* are too firmly entrenched in our culture."

"You're right, uncle," Samia agreed. "But I'm encouraged by statements made by Muslim people with vision, like Salman Rushdie. I don't remember his exact words, but he suggested that *Sharia* could be modified from its seventh century beginnings to the needs of men and women today, and that even divine dogma must be *compatible* with modern society."

"Samia," said Abdul-Raheem, "your views are one-sided. You talk only about the good things that happened to Western women, but you omit to mention the bad ones? What about the marked deterioration in morality in the West which happened because women and men were allowed to mix so freely? What about the scores of illegitimate children born during this time? Is this what we want for our Muslim families?"

"Those few illegitimate births were the least of the problems of the nation at that time," Samia snapped back.

"I cannot believe that I'm hearing this from a Muslim Arab woman!" Abdul-Raheem said, shaking his head slowly.

"A Muslim Arab woman with fresh, modern thinking, instead of one with a fossilized brain!" Samia retorted. "At least the modern world has abandoned the double standards that impose chastity on one half of society, while permitting the other half to have four wives and countless other conquests across the globe!"

"Who says that I approve of that? It, too, is sinful."

Samia continued, "So, when did we last hear about a married man being stoned to death? All I hear is laughter and applause for his sexual prowess!"

"To be fair, though, this is also true of my own Christian community," Sam interjected. "Except that we don't have any of your Draconian forms of punishment. Otherwise, the Lebanese would need to have a lot of stones!"

Everyone laughed, putting an end to the tension that had filled the room moments earlier. They decided to end the evening there and meet another time. It was late in any case.

After the others had left, Saleh turned to Samia and whispered, "I'm so proud of you and your ideas, Samia."

"I don't think they've made the slightest difference to Abdul-Raheem's mindset, though, uncle!"

"But there are many, even more rigid, people like him."

"Well, if you think there's hope, uncle, I'm willing to continue coming to these meetings. After this evening, I wasn't so sure."

"Excellent!" said Saleh, smiling.

Chapter 10
On Education in the Arab World

Back at the café for their next meeting, Sam was the first to speak.

"Our discussion last week raised quite a few issues. How about we talk about possible solutions this time? What do you think, Professor?"

Saleh spoke slowly, "Well, it goes without saying that we need education. But it should be modern education, where all opinions are considered. Also, we need to accept that it'll take decades.

"Those of us who are old enough might remember the system in place fifty years ago – where six-year-old children were expected to learn, by heart, the first segment of the Quran with its ten-line *surahs*, and then to regurgitate them back to the teacher, whose only claim to education was that he, too, learnt the Quran by heart!

"The *surahs* became longer each year, and of course, more challenging to memorize. But if we made the slightest mistake, the teacher would whack us on our palms!

"But look at our schools now; there's much less emphasis on rote learning, and more on math, geography and history. So, change is happening, but only because our parents have realized that their children need to study engineering, economics or dentistry if they want to earn a good living, and definitely if they want to work abroad.

"Education will also lead to sounder economics, which will benefit universal modern education, which means that those countries which have oil will get a supply of local technologists, engineers and designers, which should increase production and reduce its relative cost, thus increasing profit. Hopefully, that will benefit the many, not just the rulers."

"That's exactly right," Sam agreed. "So far, we've been consumers, some more than others depending on wealth. But even the more developed Arab countries can't manufacture anything. They can't make their own shoes, socks, shavers or hair dryers, or even their combs and paper towels."

"It won't last, all this wealth from fossil fuels. People are talking about the environment now. The world is changing its energy economics rapidly," Samia argued. "You see it in Europe especially. The hills of Spain are dotted with thousands of windmills generating clean, cheap power. That will lead, according to the supply and demand, to a drop in oil prices, and potentially would leave the world's sheikhdoms impoverished, not immediately, but after a while, unless they also harness solar power, of which they have plenty, and wind power where it occurs."

"But how's that going to happen?" Abdul-Raheem asked. "It seems to me that with all the new mouths to feed, every year, the world will need more, not less, fuel because there's a steady increase in the number of cars and airplanes, for a start."

"That's an area I have read a lot about," Samia responded. "If we find cheaper and cleaner alternatives to petrol, that's when it'll happen. We shouldn't underestimate public awareness of the environment, and caring about the health aspects, especially from the younger generation. The development of solar and wind power is already underway, and will only increase."

"But apart from wealth, will the Arabs ever achieve that degree of intellectual maturity that will persuade them to drastically modify their educational curricula?" Sam asked. "Are they ever going to teach their children that all those Islamic conquests, of which they are so very proud, were nothing but aggression against their neighbors to persuade them, or even force them, to adopt Islam as their religion? Are they going to ask: what if the Greek and Roman empires, and more recently, the European empires, had done the same thing to us, to spread their religion?"

Abdul-Raheem protested, "But that's exactly what they did do. We only conquered the adjacent countries – Persia, Egypt and Syria. They crossed the oceans to conquer Africa, they went all the way to Asia to conquer the Philippines, India, Vietnam, and they even conquered North and South America, Australia and New Zealand. And they decimated their peaceful indigenous populations. Even civilized Denmark! Are you aware that it conquered Greenland? And what about the Norwegians who dish out the annual Nobel Peace Prize? Did they not conquer Britain? So, let's stop this self-flagellation, to prove that we are civilized."

Sam responded, "You pose an important question, my friend. But those European marauders did not force the conquered nations to convert."

Abdul-Raheem replied, "It would've been better if they had. The Arabs were kinder in my opinion. They gave the conquered people a choice: conversion or paying taxes to ensure being protected."

Sam challenged him, "And why should the conquered people pay to be protected? That would be the duty of the government of the day, including the conquerors."

"I disagree," Abdul-Raheem replied. "The children of the Muslims would die in those wars, and that's a huge price to pay. The conquered Christians had to contribute their fair share, and they did it with money. The Muslims had to pay *Zakat.* I think that's a lesser price to pay."

"But the Muslims had no business going there in the first place. If they chose to do that, then they were responsible for any consequences."

"They went to spread the word of God."

"And who on earth invited them to do so? Why can't we, a thousand years later, at last concede that those wars were wrong, unprovoked and unjustified? The Spaniards were quite happy in their country, and had no desire or reason to learn the Quran.

Saleh had a suggestion. "You know, I have an idea! Wouldn't it be a fantastic PR move, if the Muslim Arabs simply issued an apology to the descendants of those nations for conquering them, and set an example for those who created the British, French, Belgian and American empires? Last week, I watched a video recording of a young Saudi man speaking very freely in a group of about thirty other Saudi men. He was saying things I never imagined to hear said in his country."

"Such as?" Sam asked.

Saleh said, "I recall him saying things like:

– *'We, in the Kingdom, have a strong tendency to not accept the other, whether inside or outside the country. If we go back thirty or forty years, back to the speeches of our officials, we would find that they are full of negative things about the infidels and apostates.'*

– *'The educational curricula have planted in our minds hatred for apostates, and people like those. I never heard any of our Imams participate in a civilized debate.'*

– *'Children grow up in our families, but never get the chance to express themselves. Those in charge can do whatever they want – the school teacher, the university professor, the government minister.'*

– *'I'm not optimistic at all, because all these bad habits and traditions are deep rooted in our society.'"*

Sam agreed, "I, too, was stunned by a video of an interview on TV. The program presenter asked his guest about the role of *Imams* in society, and about any problems he saw with it. So, the guest said, *'Islamic government by an Imam is not acceptable to any sane person. If any such imam came to me and claimed that he can rule over me, in the name of Allah, I would ask him why he thinks he has that right. We want to govern ourselves.'* The host asked him, *'Are you saying that a nation cannot have a religion?'* And he said, *'That's right. A nation is like a legal entity or a business corporation. It cannot have a religion.'*

Samia joined the conversation, "Thank you for sharing that detailed interview. I liked one TV interview with a woman who had the Gulf accent of Kuwait. It was only a couple of minutes long, but very interesting. It went something like this:

Host: But some people would say that the Quran and the pronouncements of Muhammad (hadeeth) are more important than the constitution? Guest: Any citizen who believes that would constitute a danger to the nation. His loyalty would not be to Kuwait, and he might be willing to commit treason against the country. We use the laws of the land to organize the people of that land. Host: So, you are advocating the separation of the church from the state, as the Europeans do? Guest: Yes, although I don't expect to have an easy or quick success doing that. But if we don't start, we will not progress.

Saleh said, "We seem to watch a lot of this type of TV show these days, especially those that criticize our dictators, the main cause of our decline, and the ones who can so easily eliminate us. I also watched a TV show called *Everything is for Sale!* The speaker was an Egyptian lawyer who said,

'When you allow a loser to control the country, he is bound to let it drown. If you want to achieve success, you need to find an educated man, someone who understands economics, not some soldier whose only expertise is war and fighting. These soldiers are the ones who ruined the country, and who imposed hunger on the people. The middle class is gone. But where are the billions we received from the Gulf countries? This man needs a psychiatrist. Even if he was sent to us by Allah, I still don't want him.'"

Sam spoke, "Well, it's *my* turn to tell you about the video I saw, a great clip of only one minute by a turbaned man, saying, with an Iraqi accent,

'Illiteracy is widespread. Ignorance, poverty, and disease are all over the nation. All, while every Friday, from the pulpits of the mosques you hear the same refrain: Please, Allah, destroy the enemies of Islam.'"

Samia offered an opinion, "That's encouraging to hear, and makes me begin to feel optimistic. But the question, gentlemen, is still whether the Arab's oil wealth will lead to prosperity or decline. You've seen with your own eyes that, in spite of the influx of Gulf riyals, Egypt, a country of one hundred million people, has been going from one crisis to another. Just think about the number of attempted assassinations against their leaders, or about the actual successful ones such as Sadat. Besides, that term is a misnomer, because the oil does not really belong to the Arabs. It belongs to a very small number of Gulf hereditary dictatorships."

Saleh spoke, "I thought about that often enough when I was working in the Gulf area, and saw the massive construction going on in places like Dubai and Doha. The rulers there have been well organized and have listened to good economic advice. At the same time, they did not allow the religious extremists to interfere with their development plans. Now their tourist industry, for one, has taken giant steps forward. I mean Dubai airport is one of the most organized, and yet friendly, in the world. I think their decision to cater to European tourists, and transit passengers, resulted in success. They did not let the Islamists impose Islamic traditions on their beaches or in their hotels."

Samia asked, "But will it last in the long term?"

Saleh responded, "I think so. Dubai has now eclipsed all the other seaports and airports in the region. That income is no longer dependent on what is under the sand, but on what is above the sand. Besides, oil will not be there forever, and the world is switching to renewable non-polluting energy sources. Some countries have started harnessing the power of the sea. And the largest solar powered battery in the world has just been built in Western Australia. So, when the demand for oil drops, prices will drop too. But production costs will not drop. Thus, the profit margin will be more severely reduced."

Sam asked, "So, what will happen then?"

Samia said, "Those who thought that oil would last forever will get a major shock and will have to tighten their belts. In a way, that's good for the region."

Abdul-Raheem asked, "How?"

"I think two things will happen," Samia predicted. "First, this current arrogance of wealth will disappear. More importantly, governments will need to collect taxes to run the country. If they collect taxes, they become answerable to their people. So, this complete hereditary dictatorship will gradually become democratized. And the young, educated, but poor people, will clamor for change."

Sam commented, "And that's a good thing – at last! I am really looking forward to that."

Saleh said, "But there's also the Egyptian model of severe poverty, unemployment and rampant corruption which can prepare the country for brutal military dictatorship."

Abdul-Raheem opined, "But this is one situation when *Sharia* law can help."

Saleh said, "I don't think so. We have seen this already. Under such circumstances, you'll always find groups of opportunists, who will serve the dictator, however brutal he might be, in order to ensure that they have privileges, which their education and responsibilities can't create. So, they become informers, enforcers and abject worshippers of the dictator."

Abdul-Raheem said, "But that happens in any nation and any culture."

Saleh agreed, "Absolutely! The Muslims and Arabs have no monopoly over corruption. And their leaders have no monopoly over dictatorship."

Sam recalled, "I remember what a psychiatrist friend of mine told me. He said that the enjoyment one gets from absolute, unfettered power over others is of the magnitude of the pleasure of orgasm! Only it lasts much, much, longer!

Certainly, longer than mine!" Sam looked at Samia to see if she was offended, but to his relief, she was not.

Samia said, "For God's sake, this is the twenty-first century!"

Saleh countered, "The twenty-first century might exist in Europe, Japan and India, but it certainly doesn't in our miserable countries, where we have learnt by heart to obey Allah, the Messengers, and all those who are in charge of us!"

"I totally agree," Samia declared. "This specific instruction is so crucial, and so destructive of democracy, that I wish it never happened, because it has been used, re-used, and in fact abused, by all those rulers and dictators, and even by cruel older family members, to extract blind obedience from us."

Chapter 11
Advice from Adonis

The following week, the four friends met again. Sam started off by asking if anyone had watched the interview of the famous Syrian writer, Adonis.

The other three looked puzzled.

"It was fantastic!" Sam enthused. "It was only five minutes long, but priceless. The TV host asked Adonis about the future of the Arab nation. This is, more or less, what he said, 'There are many problems facing the Arabs. I have said in the past, and I repeat now that we are in a state of extinction! We are neither in a state of revolution or of sleep. But we are like fish in a lake, eating each other with absolute viciousness. You might be killed in the name of nationalism or religion or in the name of the tribe. There is no hope for the Arabs, unless by some miracle, they manage to get out of this vicious cycle of being hostages to history. There's a new book by that name, which I read very recently, by Elie Nasrallah, a Canadian of Lebanese origin, that urges the Arabs to wake up from their infatuation with their past glory. Such freedom from their past history over fourteen centuries must be radical and complete. It should be replaced by a new society based on the rule of law, with emancipation of women, and the development of freedom and independent free thinking, away from any tribalism or sectarianism or religion.' Then the host asked Adonis 'Do you believe that Islam is facing a problem?' His response was, 'Of course it is. Islam, as a divine message finished when Muhammad died. At that point it ceased to be a message. It was in competition with other ideologies. It became a means for acquiring power, starting with the first caliphate. So, it was not surprising that all four caliphs after Muhammad were murdered. The same fighting continued throughout the Umayyad dynasty, and the Abbasid dynasty which followed. More recently, we had the Ottoman Empire, which ruled over the Arabs for four centuries. Imagine, a worthless empire like that ruling the Arabs for that long. Who is Turkey? What is the Ottoman Empire but a power known for violence, terror and murder? How can Islam possibly stand up to the Ottomans, when the Muslims are so fragmented until this day? Right up to this moment, the leaders of the Muslims, and you know who they are, are imposing their own rule, and it's not at all the rule of the Azhar Mosque.'

The host then asked, 'One could argue that Islam, as a religion and a way of life, does exist, and is able to survive, but for the extremists, and the subdivisions of Islamic sects?'

Adonis replied, 'We are still a bunch of tribes, living the dreams of the conquests of the past. We never left that fantasy behind. I have repeatedly called for the building of a single modern civil society. Can you name me one such Arab civil society today? Perhaps one single one emerging in Tunisia. And yet Tunisia has declared that Islam is the religion of the state! What does that imply? Islam should be a religion for the individual only, not the religion of the state. If we cannot bring ourselves to accepting that, there will simply be no progress.'"

Samia intervened, "This is absolutely wonderful! This conversation should be heard by all Arabs."

Saleh asked, "So, when are the Arabs going to wake up?"

Samia replied, "Never! But I must add that I'm quite impressed with the Tunisians, who defied the extremists and recently voted to allow Muslim women to marry non-Muslim men of their choice."

Saleh said, "Last week we talked about the Arab millionaires of the Gulf, living in the midst of mostly destitute Arab populations. But there's yet another factor that divides the Arabs into camps, and that's education. Perhaps that's the reason why Lebanon stands out among the Arab countries,

Maybe we can learn from Sam what he thinks the future holds for Lebanon's numerous religious sects."

"I don't know how we can bring those warring religious factions together," Sam reluctantly responded. "In 1870, before the Sykes-Picot catastrophe of dividing the Arab world between the British and the French empires, William Thomas said that, although the Lebanese live so close to each other, they jealously guard their separate identities. The *Sunnis* reject the *Shiites* and despise the Druze. And all three groups hate the Christians. The Greek Orthodox hate the Catholics, the Maronites hate everybody, and everyone hates the Jews. He said he couldn't think of another nation in this situation. So, has anything changed in one hundred and forty years?"

Samia responded, "Would you believe? I am actually optimistic about Lebanon."

"Really?" Sam asked. "Despite all this sectarian fragmentation?"

"*Because* of the fragmentation!"

"Pray, explain!"

"This is how I see it. Fear of the unknown, including unknown people, is natural and is part of self-preservation. It would be important for a person lost in a forest, for example, to avoid an animal that might kill him. So, when such a person wanders into an area of the forest, and sees a canine type of animal, he's not sure if it is a dog, a wolf or a fox. But if he's familiar with the behaviour of the dog, he's unlikely to be scared. That familiarity with the animal can be very reassuring. So, I'm saying that Muslims have seen the behaviour of Christians in Lebanon, and have seen them in the marketplace, or walking to their churches, perhaps holding hands with their women, and have seen Christians paying respect to effigies of Jesus and celebrating their holy days. They have lived with all that for years and know that they have nothing to fear. And vice versa."

Sam replied, "I see what you mean. Similarly, when Christian Lebanese see huge menacing hordes of Muslim men pouring out of a mosque, after Friday prayers, they're not alarmed by a potential attack or confrontation, because they have seen that many a time, and know that there is no danger at all. It's just a huge crowd of hungry men rushing home to have lunch!"

Saleh agreed, "In fact we should go out of our way to familiarize our children with the customs of other groups, so that they never suspect those groups of ill intentions or possible attack. And it does not apply to religions only. It's the same with race, as when a white American man finds himself lost in a black neighborhood and begins to imagine being held up at gunpoint, or worse."

"There's the saying 'familiarity breeds contempt'," said Samia, making quotation marks in the air. "But here, in this case, I'm saying that familiarity brings trust, and banishes suspicion. That's why intermarriage, which is the deepest form of getting to know one another, should be encouraged, in my opinion. It's happening in large numbers, in any case. We've all heard the expression 'sleeping with the enemy'. I think we should encourage our children to sleep with the so-called enemy, because it's only an enemy in our imagination. You know, I read about a small group in Canada, called 'Mixed Couples' where all the members have partners of a different religion or a different race. What a great idea! And the best thing is that they're all encouraged to bring their children with them to their meetings or their barbeques."

Abdul-Raheem added, "But we also need to remind ourselves that, when in Rome, to do as the Romans do. That's why I find it offensive when some European tourists do not respect the customs of the host country, like eating in public during *Ramadan*."

Samia countered, "What about when we see Muslim women in Europe completely covered except for two tiny holes for the eyes, in that oppressive burqa. Somehow, we don't see our own faults."

Saleh said, "Well, I can tell you a real story, where I was an unwitting witness. I was in Canada on a visit years ago, when an old school mate of mine invited me to have *Eid* dinner at his house. He offered to pick me up from my hotel. On the way home, he said he needed to make a stop. To my amazement, we stopped at a farm and he collected a live sheep! He told me that he was planning to slaughter the sheep in his bathroom so that we could eat fresh meat, as he put it! Needless to say, he had no license to do this, so I warned him against it, but he laughed it off. I was horrified but decided not to leave. It was a terrible and gruesome thing to do, and most definitely against the law. But he just laughed about it."

Samia blurted, "How gruesome!"

Sam added, "I think the worst intercultural problems are those that stem from double standards, or the impression of double standards."

Saleh asked, "Like what?"

Sam responded, "Like a Muslim man being able to marry a Christian or a Jewish woman, but not the other way around, because if she did she would be labelled an apostate. That's tantamount to execution."

Samia added, "In fact that was my own situation!"

Sam answered flippantly, "I didn't know that, Samia. So, that means it isn't too late for us? We'd make a great couple!"

Samia snapped back, "Stop your nonsense, Sam! Be serious, for a change!"

Abdul-Raheem could not help laughing, but said, "This rule is simply to protect the children, who must follow their fathers' religion."

Samia replied, "But why should they? Especially when we hear that in Judaism, they follow their mothers, which makes sense, because the mother's influence is so huge. Look how Trump's daughter, Ivanka, had to become Jewish in order to marry Jared Kushner."

Abdul-Raheem replied, "There you are! It's simpler in Islam. The woman does *not* have to convert! She can keep her faith, but the children must be brought up as Muslims. What's wrong with that? Just like Kushner's kids."

Saleh added, "The Egyptian poet, Hafez Ibrahim, wrote that 'the mother is her child's school'."

Abdul-Raheem explained, "Just as the Jews have their own *Halakhah*, we have our *Sharia* rules."

"But it's sad that the Muslim woman is the consistent loser," Samia countered. "I heard an Algerian woman on TV say, 'in Muslim society, a woman is like a refrigerator, providing food and drink to the man, whenever he feels hungry or thirsty. The only solution is for our society to abandon Islam.'"

Abdul-Raheem snapped back, "That's totally unacceptable! Let the world evolve gradually. That rule was very useful to Muslims during the Muslim invasions in Egypt, Persia and Spain, where those armies ended up marrying mostly Christian women."

Samia jumped in, "The question is: Why on earth did the Muslim armies attack whole nations and empires which did not threaten them?"

Abdul-Raheem replied, "This is ancient history, Samia, but those wars managed to spread Islam far and wide."

Samia continued, "So, those concubines paid the price of those wars by losing their husbands to the swords of the marauding Muslim armies; and on top of that they lost the religions of their ancestors, and also found their own children being brought up as Muslims. How do you think they felt about all that? What if the mostly Catholic French army did exactly the same to the Algerians?"

Abdul-Raheem replied, "But the Europeans did that and worse with the indigenous populations of North and South America. And Alexander the Great conquered so much of Asia and, no doubt, committed many atrocities."

Samia continued, "This question keeps coming up. So, by what right *did* the Muslims invade Spain? And what if the French gave themselves the same rights with the populations of North Africa, like a choice between conversion to Catholicism, or taxes linked to religion or to a bullet, given that swords are no longer in fashion? And what if the French troops considered all Muslim women in North Africa legitimate prey? After all, they were mostly horny young recruits."

Abdul-Raheem snapped back, "You don't need to invent imaginary scenarios. The Europeans did exactly that with the

77

indigenous people of North and South America. They also pillaged their wealth and changed their cultures – even criminalized their using their own language, and sexually abused their boys, never mind their girls. Like in Canada, which is considered today one of the champions of human rights."

Samia answered, "But they've confessed their crimes, and apologized, of late."

Abdul-Raheem said, "So, we're agreed that every epoch in history has its abusers, and it wasn't the Arabs or the Muslims alone. And going back into history all the way to Alexander the Great, what business had he to drag a huge army to conquer Persia three centuries before Christ? It was simply an expansionist war. What about Julius Caesar? Same thing, I would say. The Quran itself refers to this pattern where it says that the days, of success I presume, are shared by different nations, at different times.

Samia said, "You mean the *ayah* that says *tilkal ayyamu nudawiluha bainan naas?*"

Abdul-Raheem said, "Wow! I never thought for a moment that you would know that! I'm really impressed, Samia."

Saleh said, "So am I, most impressed! Fortunately, the spread of education and all these new scientific discoveries have diminished man's dependence on Holy Scriptures of all nations, and I'd expect that to continue at an accelerated pace. As Muslim children, we read that the stars were sometimes used to hit the devils, but we now know a lot more about the stars and the planets and the whole universe. Indeed, some very wealthy people, I hear, have booked their flights to certain destinations in outer space. And when that happens, what if we discover that there is vegetation there, which would imply that there is water, and energy? And if there is vegetation, then, are there animals of any kind? Are there humans, perhaps? If all that transpires, will anyone still believe in God?"

Abdul-Raheem responded, "What a rich and florid imagination you have, Professor! Sounds like a fanciful dream."

Saleh answered, "May I remind you that, until recently, people were talking about simple things like the eclipse of the moon or the sun as a divine phenomenon. And now we can predict the coming eclipses to the nearest minute or even second. That's why I am confident that our grandchildren will shun our ways and will believe in proven scientific fact far more readily than we've done. And there will be another important development, I believe more and more Islamic scholars will begin to subscribe to these scientific theories and will witness them with their own eyes. And once that happens, they will influence the less educated public."

Abdul-Raheem asked, "But even if these scientists did reach and establish camps in outer space, how will they come back?"

Saleh said, "The same way that Yuri Gagarin came back, and all the others that followed him. I'm not sure why you asked the question. All you need is a 'vehicle' that can escape the gravitational pull of the earth, in order to leave, and have the ability to gradually descend to earth without burning."

Samia added, "Our world is scoring very rapid scientific successes, and I read somewhere that the changes in the next fifty years will be many times the advances of the past fifty. I doubt if people, including the trailing Muslims, will be interested in who is *Sunni* or Shiite, or even Muslim, which is exactly what I'd like to see. It'll be like the current interest in Christianity. Frankly, people will be saying 'who cares?'. And the best part of it all is that the Arabs and Muslims will probably start to use logic in their discussions, because logic comes from having a scientific base, in my experience. I can just see it now. Four Arabs like us sitting in a circle, doing something they've never done before; *actually listening* to each other, and then responding politely and using logic and science, because they know that the old system of *takfeer* is gone, and the dreaded label of apostasy no longer scares the hell out of them."

Saleh continued, "The differences between the way we discuss our problems, and the way the West does it, are stark. Any challenge or even questioning of *Sharia* or the pronouncements of the Prophet, or even of a local *Imam*, is met with consternation or insults if not physical violence. And soon the label of apostasy is bestowed on whoever does that. You even see that among so-called intellectuals on TV, who raise their voices to drown out their opposition, or who throw shoes across the table because shoes have this bizarre significance in the Arab world of being filthy, which of course they are not in the West. When I see this, I don't know whether to laugh at or cry for my people."

Abdul-Raheem agreed, "It's so embarrassing! In fact, it's quite shameful. I've stopped watching these Arabic debates, because, as an Arab, I feel so humiliated. I feel I want to change my name... but... I can't."

Saleh added, "There are a few people who have the moral courage to try to change things for the better, but I imagine that most of them don't want to run the gauntlet of assassination. I mean most people would ask themselves, 'Is it worth it?' So, the question is why those extremists want to kill our opportunity for progress in the twenty-first century."

Saleh continued with his explanation. "It's natural to be wary of new ideas, new systems or even new neighbors. It's even happened to us. Think about all the new technology, which is so frustrating for us to learn, but which our grandchildren know backwards. But the dangerous part is when Muslims believe that it's their sacred duty to kill those who come up with ideas that challenge Islam, and when they believe that they will go to paradise if they kill those who promote such ideas, because it's part of *Jihad*."

Sam spoke, "I agree. Progressive people need safe space to discuss if not promote their ideas and beliefs without fear. That's why such discussions cannot be left in the hands of *Imams* or priests."

Saleh said, "Let's try to copy Turkey, which is heading in a relatively secular direction. As long ago as 1877, Turkey adopted civil laws that replaced the *Sharia* ones, as a result of which, it made significant progress. It is now applying to join the European Union, I believe. We also need to remember that some of these *Sharia* laws are based on *hadith*, which is the sayings of the Prophet, which in turn were written by people other than the Prophet because he was illiterate. It seems that the person who collected and verified this *hadith* was a man called Bukharee, from the Caucasus, who collected seven thousand of them, even though Arabic was not his native tongue. So, there is some room for error."

Abdul-Raheem replied, "Doctor Saleh, I like your idea of following the Turkish initiative, because Turkey is a prospering country. In fact, I take this as proof that Islam does not impede progress. Don't you agree? It's only a small minority of Muslims who stand in the way of progress or use violence to do so. But I am also impressed with your knowledge about the *hadith*."

Sam joined in, "But what's your evidence that violent reactions are only committed by a small minority, when we witness such violence almost daily on TV? Even though I didn't read your Quran, I still remember one verse that is used to encourage violence for the sake of Allah. You know it, I'm sure; it's the one that says *'do not think that those who were killed in the service of Allah are dead; for they are alive, thriving with their God.'"

Abdul-Raheem added, "There is no doubt that the Arab Spring, which started in Tunis on the 18th December 2010, was a unique phenomenon for the Arab world. People were desperate to rid themselves of dictatorship, and since their rulers never allowed normal democracy to exist, young men and women had to organize the uprisings themselves. But when it came to running a government, the Islamic organizations were the only ones who had the manpower and structure in place to govern. And most people were happy with that change, in fact, with any change."

Saleh added, "But, because of sectarianism, rampant in several Arab countries, conflicts soon erupted. Also because of natural vying for power, as happened in Yemen, Iraq and Syria. And so, the Arabs proved, yet again, that they cannot learn from past mistakes, so they fought each other with unprecedented ferocity and they tried to use Islam as the law of the land."

Sam added, "Even though I am Christian, I had some hope that the Muslim brotherhood might succeed in establishing a stable and inclusive government. But the military apparatus never gave them a chance. They returned with a vengeance, possibly encouraged by colonial powers, or by our so-called 'Arab brothers'."

Saleh agreed, "I agree with all that. But I also learnt about the financial aspects of all this. I watched a TV interview with a Canadian professor, named Stein, who told her interviewer that the army would intervene to annul the Tahrir Square revolution, simply because the armed forces owned and managed more than one third of the economy of Egypt. And she proved to be absolutely correct in her prediction. And here we are with yet another military general ruling the largest Arab country with an iron fist, having put the elected president in jail. Why? Because the military dictator has the support of so many Arab and non-Arab governments, both democratic and dictatorial."

Samia said, "It reminds me of what Henry Kissinger once said – that a small number of very wealthy states have managed to influence what is happening in the world. Let us also remember that the rate of unemployment among the youth in these Arab countries was about sixty percent. So, people have priorities. Like food, for example!"

Abdul-Raheem added, "That's a phenomenon which is common to many poor and populous countries. Too many mouths to feed, and not enough jobs, or very poorly paid jobs. Of course, they produce large families because of high infant mortality. So, couples produce large families knowing ahead of time that some will die, but then enough will survive in order to look after the ageing parents later. And with that comes illiteracy, or poor education. And the two feed off each other."

Samia added, "But Islamic tradition is part of the cause, for the Prophet is reported to have said, 'Multiply and increase your numbers, for I want to brag about you among other nations on the day of resurrection'. In other words, no birth control!"

Sam suggested, "It's getting late. But I feel that we've had a great discussion today. My summary would be that petrol has been a boon for the Arabs, but only for the privileged ten percent of them. I recall when Gamal Abdul-Nasser of Egypt changed the term Arab oil to The Ruler's Oil. He proved to be right on that score."

Saleh suggested, "That's why he was assassinated!"

Abdul-Raheem asked, "I thought it was a natural death."

Saleh snapped, "Yes, as natural as that of Yasser Arafat!"

The discussion ended, with an agreement to meet at the Café Mocha, two weeks later.

Chapter 12
Predictions

The four friends settled round a square table at the Café Mocha, with their large cups.

Abdul-Raheem started, "I have to tell you that I had a major debate with my eldest son, last week, about what is happening in the Middle East, especially about Yemen, where we lived for several years. I was surprised at the depth of his knowledge about politics and human rights, and even about religion."

Saleh asked, "That sounds like a good thing. Did you not think so?"

Abdul-Raheem replied, "Yes, I did. But it took me by surprise, because I didn't think he would have much knowledge about social change and politics at his age. But then he watches the BBC and all sorts of other channels, and surfs the internet. He has his own laptop, you know."

Samia said, "Welcome to the future, Abdul-Raheem! You're no longer in the oppressive Arab world, where all TV stations sing the praises of the dictators. These kids, my daughter Tina included, have a voracious appetite for knowledge and news, and they want to make up their own minds. No more spoon feeding by the parents or the teachers or the *Imams*."

Abdul-Raheem replied, "That's good. But I do worry that they may overdo it and acquire harmful thoughts and ideas."

Saleh jumped in, "I see it as a good omen. And, eventually, you'll have to decide whether you want your children to grow up to be Yemenis or British. You brought them here to give them a better chance, didn't you?"

"Yes, indeed. I know that they'll be influenced by their new environment. I just hope that they keep the values of their religion. But, this time, I have burnt my boats! They're already blending into this society. They will hardly be Arabs in future."

Samia said, "Like me with Tina, you will have no choice, my friend. In any event, I think they're lucky, because the Arabs will eventually recognize that their abundant oil was a disaster. When they found oil, they went from nothing to getting drunk on 'petrol power'. But instead of putting their new-found wealth into nation building by investing in education, technology and democracy, they hired millions of cheap laborers from Asia to do absolutely every job. One of those jobs included bringing up their children, some of whom grew up not able to speak the language of their parents. It's become so widespread that even the Kuwaiti Minister of Health, Doctor Al-Awadhi, warned Kuwaitis about it during the Gulf War."

Sam added, "I think we're lucky to have among us an expert on banking and economics. What are your predictions for the future, Samia?"

Samia responded, "I must confess that I am no expert, but I do keep an eye on these issues. Look guys, when we want to evaluate and compare financial affluence in different nations, we use the GDP per capita values…"

Abdul-Raheem asked, "GDP? What's that?"

Samia explained, "Sorry, that's the gross domestic product per person in the population in any one country. So, let's take some examples. The figure for the USA is $57,000. The Kingdom of Saudi Arabia is close behind the Americans with $54,000, and Canada's is $40,000. Let's look at our countries. Egypt's is $12,000, but Yemen's is only $2500, but there is one that is even worse, and that's Somalia with only $400. I don't remember Lebanon's, but guess which country is at the very top because of its very small population?"

As there was no answer, Samia answered the question herself. "Qatar with a figure of $130,000," she said.

Sam remarked, "What a huge range of figures!"

Samia added, "But the situation is even worse than what these figures suggest, because they are averages. That means that they assume that the GDP is divided equally among the population of a country. But it isn't divided equally. Which means that the very poorest people in Somalia, for example, earn even less than $400 per year, that's a dollar a day. Can you imagine that?"

Abdul-Raheem said, "This is terrible. I'm sure that part of the reason is the endemic corruption in the Middle East."

"Corruption isn't only in poor countries like Somalia and Yemen; it's widespread," Samia elaborated, "but the siphoning of millions into the foreign bank accounts of the rulers is corruption to the extreme. The ruler of your country, Abdul-Raheem, was believed to have a few *billion* dollars in his foreign accounts, while the people suffered famine and disease. And let's not forget that each dictator or prince has his circle of very close friends and protectors, and they, too, would get a cut."

Abdul-Raheem explained, "In our country, it's well known that the president encourages his ministers to steal public funds because he knows that, if they do, they won't criticize him or rebel against him."

Sam asked, "Is it true that in Yemen, the young played a major role in the uprising?"

Abdul-Raheem responded, "Indeed! The young were active in all countries that went through the Arab Spring upheaval. But Yemen has a relatively high percentage of children because of a high fertility rate. As someone said to me, the Yemenis breed like rabbits!"

Everyone laughed.

Abdul-Raheem continued, "It was very sad, because so many of them were murdered in cold blood, after being accused of being 'terrorists' by the president and his ministers of national security and foreign affairs, who tried to persuade world leaders of that falsehood."

Saleh asked, "Is it true that thousands of innocent civilians were killed by indiscriminate bombing by the Saudi air force?"

Abdul-Raheem responded, "That's what we Yemenis hear all the time."

Saleh asked, "But why? I thought they were there to defend civilians?"

"Every time we ask that question, we hear that well-known American excuse of 'collateral damage'," Abdul-Raheem said.

"Very puzzling!" Sam added.

"In Yemen, there is a well-known story about the founder of the House of Saud. His name was Abdul-Aziz bin Saud. He was a sheikh who got permission from the British Prime Minister, Winston Churchill, to declare himself king – just like that! So, he gathered together his numerous children, by numerous wives, and warned them that the Yemenis, because of their much larger population, might one day destroy their kingdom. He urged them to always suspect and watch them very carefully."

Sam asked, "So, what do you think will happen in Yemen?"

Abdul-Raheem hesitated, then answered, "I have very little hope for Yemen. There's too much tribalism, sectarianism and poverty. Plus, there's a huge number of weapons, estimated to be two weapons per person, in a population of twenty-five million!"

Saleh added, "I am afraid I do share this very pessimistic prediction for Yemen. I think the country should go back to being separated into North and South Yemen. The southern region was much more educated, developed and democratic, and if that still holds true, it should survive better on its own. It might even be necessary for Hadhramaut to become an independent entity."

"But if that happens, we'll have too many little insignificant states," Abdul-Raheem lamented.

"And what's wrong with that? Look at the peace that has prevailed in the former Yugoslavia, since it fragmented into Serbia, Croatia and Bosnia, after being hastily put together by Tito."

"But there is strength in unity."

"Not when it comes to the Arabs. For one simple reason."

"What's that?"

"Because the Arabs can't negotiate," Saleh explained. "In order to negotiate, you have to listen to the point of view of the other side, something which the Arab mind isn't accustomed to. It's always 'my way or the highway'! Negotiating in Arab culture is often considered a sign of weakness, and the sense of honour and shame is so paramount in our culture. It would be easier to commit suicide than to concede defeat."

Sam chided, "You exaggerate my friend. Everyone negotiates in the end."

Saleh replied, "I hope I'm wrong. I really do."

"So, what do you men think will happen in the end? How about you, Uncle?" Samia asked.

Saleh answered hesitantly, "You won't like what I have to say, I warn you. But if you insist, I'll answer. Let's start with Palestine. There will *never* be a sovereign Palestine! There will be a Palestinian minority within Israel. They will be second or third class, relatively uneducated, very poor, living in designated areas, just as was the case in South Africa. It will be recognized by all Arab states, with the possible exception of Kuwait and Tunisia, two very small states. None of the Arab countries will have a proper parliamentary democracy, with the possible exception of Tunisia. The *Sunni-Shiite* competition will continue unabated in all the countries where the two communities exist. Egypt will be a very highly populated, extremely poor, corrupt and totally chaotic country, still ruled by the armed forces. Turkey and Iran will continue to prosper to become the major centers of power in the Middle East. They will eventually establish diplomatic relations with Israel."

Abdul-Raheem asked, "And Yemen?"

Saleh looked surprised, then said, "You should be answering this question, not me! But I think that Yemen will split into three parts: Hadhramaut in the south east, North Yemen and South Yemen. Hujariyah, in the south, will make an attempt to join South Yemen because of sectarian reasons and also because most people in the South are descendants of families in the Taiz region, and share culture and values with them."

"Sounds like wishful thinking to me!"

"Listen, you asked me. I didn't volunteer. So, what do *you* think then?"

"I am not a clever educated man like you. I don't know."

"Neither am I," Saleh said. "There are people who make a career of making such predictions, but they usually have a politics or journalism background. The important thing is not to be afraid to say that you were wrong in your predictions and that you would be happy to revise them."

Sam commented, "I like that. But I doubt that there will be this blanket recognition of Israel, as you said."

Saleh added, "I'm not surprised that you say that. I'll tell you why. You would refrain from doing so as long as the Palestinians don't have full citizenship rights, because you believe in human rights and equality, and you saw how the Copts were treated. But the presidents of all those Arab countries are either military men or hereditary rulers, who, by definition, do *not* believe in equality, nor in human rights. They couldn't care less about the rights of Palestinians or anyone else. Yes, they may offer lip service to that for public consumption, but what's important is their actions later."

"I agree, Doctor," Abdul-Raheem said. "For example, in South Yemen, popular revolution drove the British out, and people got all excited about what they thought was freedom, only to discover that the local rulers were brutal dictators who craved power and killed anyone who stood in their way, including their own comrades and their own family members. I learnt this English saying: 'Power corrupts, and absolute power corrupts absolutely!'"

"We should redefine the word 'freedom'," Samia concluded. "There, in the Arab world, it's used to mean freedom from colonialism, because of the history of the region. But it should mean freedom of speech, of choice, of religion or lack of it, of political affiliation, and even freedom of sexual orientation. We are centuries away from that stage! It'll happen only gradually. But happen, it must."

Abdul-Raheem said, "As you know, I decided to bring up my children here for the sake of their education. But, let's be honest. There is a lot of suspicion against Muslims in the West, right here, and downright racism and xenophobia. It's all over. On the internet, in the street, on social media, even in the regular press. Why? Because the owners of the press hate us."

Saleh responded, "You are absolutely right. It's become the fashion now to demonize Muslims and Arabs. But we don't know how to defend ourselves. And when we do, it's always with bombs or by driving trucks into innocent people walking on London Bridge. How does that help?"

"Of course that doesn't help, and we should condemn it in no uncertain terms. But let me tell you how we *can* very effectively silence Islamophobia with a good example."

All eyes were on Samia.

She resumed, "I'm a bank manager as you know. Let me show you how money talks with this hypothetical story: Imagine that the city of Cardiff, where Abdul-Raheem was born, has a population of half a million, and that 10,000 of these are Arabs. The owner-publisher of the Cardiff Chronicle is a Mr. Thaicoon. He happens to hate Arabs and makes sure the Cardiff Chronicle shuns them, and demeans them at every opportunity. The Arab Association of Wales sends a delegation of three to reason with the management. At the end of the meeting, management denies any bias and tells the delegation that if the Arabs did not like the paper, they could start their own. Now, what should the Arab community do?"

"They should write letters to the paper, and complain to the local human rights commission," said Abdul-Raheem.

Nadia responded, "I knew you'd say that. But that won't work, because it would be difficult and lengthy to prove bias. But there is a guaranteed and rapid solution, which I know as a woman who deals in money. They say money talks, right? Let's imagine that the owner, Thai Coon, makes 300,000 pounds a year, and lives in great luxury. This is the net profit after deducting expenditure from revenue which consists of advertising fees and paper sales at one pound a copy. Let's say that the number of issues per year is 300, noting that the paper is not published on Sundays or public holidays. We just agreed that out of a Cardiff population of half a million, 2% that is, 10,000 are Arabs. Let's make that 2000 households with an average of 5 people per household. What do you think would happen if on ONE AGREED DAY, only 1000 Arab subscribing households cancelled the Cardiff Chronicle for that one year? You guessed it, Thai Coon's annual income will drop to zero!"

Abdul-Raheem said, "Wow!"

Samia continued, "But even if you couldn't find one thousand willing Arabs, and only 100 responded, Thai Coon's income would drop by 30,000 to 270,000 pounds. Do you think he'll like that?"

Sam looked with admiration at Samia, and said, "Brilliant! That's really brilliant, Samia. I never would have worked this out myself. And yet it is quite obvious. We need a bottle of wine, to drink to your health and brilliance."

Chapter 13
And Tina Makes Five

One week later, the group met at the home of Samia, at her invitation. There, Samia's twenty-year-old daughter, Tina, was helping her mother offer food and drinks to their guests. Tina knew her great uncle Saleh, of course, but Samia introduced her to the other two men.

Samia said, "This is my only daughter, Tina, who is studying pharmacy at the West Thames College of Science."

Sam asked, "Delighted to meet you, Tina. How are you finding the study of all those drugs?"

Tina replied, "Not too bad, although I have a huge number of Latin names to remember, together with the structure and side effects of far too many chemicals."

Sam countered, "At your age, that's not a problem. Wait until you get to my age!"

Saleh added, "Better still, wait until you're *my* age. Then you won't remember anything, not even your own name!"

Sam looked cunningly at Saleh and asked, "What did you say your name was?"

Saleh said, "Umm, umm, how soon would you like to know?"

Everyone laughed.

Sam asked Tina, "How many students are there in your class?"

Tina guessed that there were forty.

Sam continued, "Have you made any friends in class?"

Tina replied, "Yes, of course. It's a relatively small group. And we are all more or less the same age."

Sam persisted, "Mostly males?"

Tina said, "On the contrary, two thirds are girls."

Sam probed further, "Any *special* man?"

Tina blushed.

Samia intervened, "Don't pay him any attention, Love, he's just nosy! Typical Lebanese!"

Sam countered, "No, I'm not! I just want to make sure that she's making some man happy – unlike some people I know! I mean all that beauty has to be enjoyed and appreciated."

"I'm perfectly happy precisely because I don't have to worry about some inadequate, whining man in my life!" Samia retorted.

Sam continued with his interrogation. "So, are we likely to meet this mystery man?"

Tina replied, "Actually, yes. He's picking me up soon. We're going out as a foursome."

"Great! What's his name?"

Tina replied, "Alex. He's very nice. We've been dating for six months."

Samia addressed Tina, "Thank you, my love, for helping with the tea for our guests. Alex is usually on time, isn't he? We'll have finished by the time he arrives. Give him my best."

Sam asked Samia, "So, have you met him, Samia? Is he OK? Do you approve?"

"Yes, of course. He's been here several times. He's very nice, and Tina is a very sensible girl who does not need my approval."

Abdul-Raheem joined the conversation, "Young people these days don't need the guidance of their parents. I'm lucky; my children are all under ten, but I do worry about the rapidly approaching teen tears. In this country, they don't seem to know their limits."

Samia responded, "We all want to protect our children. Indeed, it is our duty. But this is a free country that guarantees free speech, free behaviour and free belief. You can also choose where to live, what to wear and whom to associate with."

"I realize that I'll have to deal with these issues sooner or later," Abdul-Raheem said, "and that it's going to be tough. I know of people who wanted to integrate so much, that they didn't impose any restrictions. Now they regret that decision as some of the kids have started doing drugs and having sex, which has caused many scandals within our community. I'm not going to be strict with my own children, but I'll also not abdicate my responsibility."

Samia responded, "All parents want to protect their children and to avoid scandal, but the decision in this country is not in the hands of the parents after a certain age. English law is very clear that boys as well as girls are free to do what they like after a certain age. So, Tina can smoke, drink, have sex or even marry a woman – if she's so inclined."

"Yes, I know, but for me there are red lines, and Islam forbids a Muslim woman from marrying a non-Muslim man, and I can't allow sex outside marriage, but I know that will be difficult."

"So, what are you going to do if your daughter defies you? Kill her like Banaz's father and uncle did? Or, drown her in a canal, like that Afghani father drowned his daughters in Canada? He actually drowned the daughters and their mother who was his first wife! He had acquired a second wife by then."

"Of course not! But I'll recruit all members of the family, and her own girlfriends to convince her that this is forbidden in Islam."

Samia replied, "My guess is that her girlfriends, being of the same age and mentality, will actually take her side of the argument. Then what?"

"Look! This is my daughter, and I want what's best for her."

"We all want what's best for our children. If she accepts that argument, well and good. But if she doesn't, she can take you to court and put you in jail if you pose a threat to her. I hope you have a good lawyer! And I hope you'll be able to defend the blatant double standards to the judge and jury."

"What double standards? I'll want my boys to do the same."

"How are you going to convince the judges that it's perfectly fine for your son to marry an infidel woman, but not for your daughter to marry a non-Muslim infidel? You'll be laughed out of court when the jury hears that you allow your sons to fornicate with whom they choose, yet you would murder your daughter for the same 'crime'."

"Christianity does not have such laws, but in Islam it is her duty as a Muslim woman to remain pure. It's our religion and these are our long-held customs."

"Once again I ask, why does it not apply to your sons then?"

"Islam allows men to do that; to marry a Christian or a Jewish girl, preferably a virgin."

"Yes I know. But why a virgin?"

"What do you mean why? To prove that no other man has touched her."

Samia repeated, "Why?"

"Do we need to go into these intimate details?"

"Not if you don't want to," Saleh said, "but you'll either have to admit that there are double standards, or you'll have to explain why it's different for a girl."

Abdul-Raheem, attempted an explanation. "It's different because the groom pays a dowry in order to marry and therefore expects to see those spots of blood on the bed sheets."

Samia protested, "But there's no such thing as a dowry these days. A boy and a girl combine their assets, establish a home and generally get on with it. But tell me, what difference do the blood spots make if there is love between the two?"

"They assure the groom that the bride will not think of anyone else but him. Thus, love is stronger."

"But the same argument could be used about the man. Or do you think that the man, like a boxer or a wrestler, needs a lot more pre-wedding training in order to do the job?"

"You're being provocative, Samia. I thought we were supposed to have a polite dialogue. In any case, I didn't write these rules. Allah ordered us to follow them, and all I am doing is following them."

"I apologize if it sounds that way to you. But I find it demeaning that *Sharia* customs – in the twenty first century – insist that a Muslim woman should be content with following such archaic rules."

"These rules have stood the test of time for Muslims who choose to follow *Sharia*. And they've kept our women chaste and faithful."

Samia hesitated, then said, "OK! Let's imagine a city in the Middle East. Take Taiz in Yemen. This city, let's assume, has a population of one hundred thousand unmarried adults, another one hundred thousand married adults, and say, three hundred thousand children. Half a million in total. Let's assume that forty percent of the unmarried male adults have regular sex, but that only ten percent of the unmarried women do. Simple mathematics suggests that either each young woman has four partners, or that there is a huge number of very busy prostitutes in town."

Abdul-Raheem looked dumbfounded, then said, "The first scenario is not possible. The second is conceivable. But… but… you're assuming that forty percent of men are sinners, which… which… which can't be correct."

Samia continued, "Which century are you living in, my friend? Look, there's nothing personal in this, and I know that nobody wants to hear it, especially in Muslim society. But show me where I am wrong, and I'll withdraw my argument."

Saleh intervened, "You know, my friends, this is a rather difficult subject to discuss. It's even more sensitive than talking about religion because it involves the taboos of honour and shame. It is especially true because Islam is considered by Muslims to be the final religion on this earth, and that causes problems for immigrants when they take this huge cultural leap from the Middle East to the UK."

"True," Abdul-Raheem agreed. "In the *surah* of *al-maidah*, the holy Quran says, 'Today I have completed your religion and showered you with blessings, and accepted Islam as your religion'."

Sam said, "Yes, I read that *surah* out of interest once. But man will never stop questioning what he does not fully understand. And that has become the norm in Western society."

Saleh added, "And the other side of the coin is that those who like and approve of the status quo will vehemently defend it. They feel safe in it. It's the only thing they've known since childhood. It's what their parents, whom they love and respect, have taught them. So, why entertain any other new foreign theories?"

"You're absolutely right, Uncle," Samia said. "The only problem I have is that there are people who will not permit me to change my allegiances, or update my knowledge, or pronounce new hypotheses. At the beginning of Islam, I can understand why conversion from Islam would be considered a huge crime, punishable by death. I'm not saying it's right, only understandable. But today with Muslims constituting 20% of the population of this globe, what's the risk? And yet, these same people have huge celebrations when a Christian or a Hindu converts to Islam. Why this one-way street?"

Abdul-Raheem offered, "There are many good reasons to convert to Islam, in my opinion."

"But you'll find that the Catholics can make the same argument, and the Sikhs, and…"

"I don't know the other religions, so I can't say. But if Islam is such a problematic religion, that demands five prayers a day, imposes fasting for a whole month every year and prohibits alcohol, how come there are so many converts to it?"

Sam answered, "I don't pretend to know, but many, if not most, of the converts are black Americans who like the important principle of equality of all Muslims. When they compare it with the horrific racial discrimination they were born into, they find refuge in it."

Abdul-Raheem added, "Also, in Islam, the relationship between the Muslim and Allah is a direct one, and not through an intermediary, such as a priest. When a Muslim prays, he is communicating with Allah one on one. It's a simple and attractive concept."

Samia asked, "But there's nothing simple or attractive about the *furoodh*, the five daily prayers. It's so disruptive. How can you schedule your day if you are expected to stop everything five times a day in order to pray? How does an MP, a nurse, a teacher, a police officer, or even a pilot do that?"

"You know very well that you can do all five sets of prayers together when you go home."

"Yes, I do know that, but it doesn't happen that way. Nowadays, people demand facilities to do their ablutions and spaces to pray at work. Airports, too, have to have prayer rooms. By contrast, in one or two Arab countries, non-Muslims are not allowed to build or buy a building to make it into a church."

Sam intervened, saying, "Talking about churches and mosques, what I've never understood is why there are four genuflexions at noon prayers, three at sunset and two at dawn."

"I don't actually know," admitted Abdul-Raheem.

Samia jumped in, "What about animal cleanliness? I've always wanted to know about that. I saw a picture on the internet of some men sitting on the floor of a mosque waiting for prayers to start. Between two of the men was a cat. The caption read 'even the cat wants to pray to God'. Would a cat really be allowed in the mosque, even though it could have brought all sorts of filth in on its paws? I imagine that a dog would have caused a riot, regardless of how clean it was."

"A dog is considered unclean – *najis* in Arabic."

"Why? There are millions of dogs here in London, all clean, groomed and well-cared for. So, from a purely scientific point of view, that doesn't make sense, does it?"

"Not everything is judged scientifically. Sometimes there are empirical rules."

"The same goes for the ban on pork. Why?"

"That's clearly banned by name in the Quran."

"Yes, I know, but why?"

"The pig is a very dirty animal."

"So are the chicken and sheep, yet millions are slaughtered in Mecca for Eid al-Fitr."

"But you can pick up worms from eating pork."

Saleh felt that he had to intervene. "Let me try to help here. Yes, it's true that pigs carry the worm, *Tuenia solium*, but cows carry an equivalent worm, called *T. Saginata*. And yet beef is allowed."

Abdul-Raheem responded, "I don't know all these scientific things. All I know is that pork is prohibited by name in the holy book, and that's good enough for me. If Allah wanted to prohibit beef too, he would have said that in the Quran. But He didn't."

Samia continued, "But we're not using our heads here. Let us think of the average father or mother, being asked these embarrassing questions by their curious six-year-old children. How are they going to answer them?"

Abdul-Raheem answered, "You know, when I was a child, I remember that my father explained things to me, and that I always trusted his word and never doubted it, and never, ever questioned him. And I'll bring up my children in that same tradition – to respect whoever is older. An Arabic proverb says, 'He who is one day older than you, is one year wiser'."

Saleh intervened, "I've got news for you, my friend. That ancient saying no longer works; certainly not here in the UK. So, unless you're planning to move back to Yemen, you'll be challenged. Your kids will get most of their information from school, from their friends, and above all, from the internet. You won't be able to stop it! So, here's a question you'll be asked by your son: Why is it that if I pass gas from below, that I am considered dirty and have to go through ablutions again before I pray? Maybe he's already asked you that?"

Abdul-Raheem said, "I'd tell him the truth, which is that cleanliness is very important when you are praying to Allah."

Saleh persisted, "Little children are honest and logical. He's likely to say to you that he's as clean as he was one minute before passing that gas. So, why do ablutions?"

Abdul-Raheem also persisted, "I'd tell him that when he passes gas he might also soil his underwear without realizing it."

"But then he'd disagree and say that he'd know if that happened. And from your own experience, you know this to be true. So, now what?"

"I'd explain that there's no harm in being extra clean, and in making sure that you are pure enough for prayers."

"You know what? I think he's likely to be put off all prayers, because you will not have convinced him. The same with menstruation. Give me a convincing scientific reason to show that it is impure."

"There, it's obvious that the woman is not clean. Therefore, she should postpone her prayers or her fasting until she is clean."

Samia butted in, "Since you're talking about women, let me tell you that there is nothing dirty about menstruation. There's bleeding for three days or so, but it's both clean and sterile blood. If that blood was contaminated, the woman would be very ill with septicemia. As a biologist, don't you agree, Uncle?"

Saleh responded, "Of course! Bacteria love blood; they thrive in it. But this is blood which is flowing outwards, out of the womb. It is a monthly natural phenomenon. Billions of women experience it regularly. Urine, too, is clean and sterile. Yes, it may have a peculiar smell, but it is not dirty. In fact, there was an Indian prime minister, called Shastri, I believe, who told the world that he drank his own urine every day – and felt better for doing so!"

"How disgusting!" Abdul-Raheem blurted. "Next you'll tell me that this Shastri man also ate his… you know what!"

"No, no! That's completely different," Saleh explained. "Feces not only stink but teem with bacteria and sometimes with parasites. That's how cholera spread like wildfire in Haiti after the earthquake, and in Yemen during the bombing of Sana'a by the Saudi Air Force. Do you know what is full of bacteria yet does not necessitate new ablutions before prayers? Saliva! So why are Muslims not required to go through ablutions after spitting? Or after blowing their noses, which is very common?"

Abdul-Raheem said, "Perhaps it's because at the time of Muhammad (May the greetings of Allah be upon him), these facts, which require a microscope, were not known."

Saleh said, "But this is what I keep returning to; why are we not allowed to modify these obsolete rules, now that our knowledge has increased?"

Abdul-Raheem admitted, "I've run out of answers, frankly, but I'm happy to follow the old rules, for the sake of my faith."

"Uncle Saleh, you forgot to mention another more recent phenomenon," Samia said. "This one involves women, of course. How many times have we seen an unsuspecting man putting his arm forwards to shake the hand of a woman he is introduced to, only to have the woman withdraw her hand abruptly, and place it on her chest, as if to say 'sorry I don't shake hands with men'."

Saleh replied, "When I asked about that, I was told the unlikely story that such handshaking may turn into sensual feeling, which would then bring about sensual reactions in the man, which in turn might cause involuntary leakage of 'certain fluids', which in turn would annul the state of cleanliness and ablution!"

Samia giggled, and said, "Now I've heard everything! I reckon that a normal handshake between two strangers is likely to last two seconds. Are we to believe that there are men in this world who would get aroused from such two-second contact? I think the whole world is laughing at us. No, I don't *think* it is, I *know* it is!"

Saleh said, "The ignorance surrounding these rituals is frankly mind-boggling. I didn't know that there was something called 'torture in the grave', until I attended a lecture in a well-known city in the Gulf, to attend a book exhibition. It was very well organized, I must say. There were many lectures and presentations by well-known international authors. One of these was a secular, female, Egyptian writer who talked, among other things, about this subject. It is supposed to happen to Muslims who do not wash their organs properly after they urinate. I assumed that she would blurt out the usual acceptance, but to my relief and surprise, she assured her audience that there was no such thing. What was even more surprising was the standing ovation she received at the end of her contribution."

Samia commented, "There's hope for the Muslims, then?"

Abdul-Raheem said, "I understand what you want to say, but all religions have their rules and their rituals too. I'm not a highly educated man like you, so I prefer to simply follow the rules, and do my best to be a good Muslim."

"For me, it's different. These rules don't concern me and don't impact my life, simply because I don't practice them," Samia said. "What I do care about, however, is my right to discuss them, to evaluate them and to criticize them if I want to. But that also applies to criticizing Buddhist and Christian rituals, too. I can't accept that challenging them deserves violence, insults or calling me an apostate, but I do feel sorry that people of other religions, or no religion, may be mocking us as a group. And because of my name and my association with Muslims, I get the same labels and the same derision. Like when I meet an Arab man, and offer my hand for a handshake, and he refuses to reciprocate. How do you think that makes me feel?"

Sam piped in, "Samia! *This* Arab man will never reject *your* hand!"

Big smiles by everyone reduced the tension in the room.

Abdul-Raheem said, "I hear you, Samia, but isn't it within my rights, by the same token, to refuse to shake hands with a woman if I feel that it compromises my religious beliefs?"

"Yes, of course," Samia replied. "That goes without saying."

Abdul-Raheem conceded, "Good. We're agreed then!"

Samia continued, "But let's imagine that you went to a comedy show at one of the theatres and saw this being enacted and everyone was laughing about it. Would that not bother you?"

Abdul-Raheem said, "Hmmm! I'm not sure. I would consider it to be in bad taste, though."

Samia replied, "But in the West, such plays are common. Most of the time the jokes are about the Scots, the Irish or the French, but the Arabs may be included soon. In fact, they *should* be targeted, in my opinion. I wish Arab comedians would start poking fun at themselves. Indians do. We should remember that Arabs poke fun at Somalis, Indians, Greeks and the British as well. So why is that OK?"

Abdul-Raheem replied, "I don't poke fun at other people, but I'm sure others do. I don't approve. It's a form of racism."

Samia countered, "So, have you written about that in the local paper or on Facebook? Have you walked in a protest demonstration on Seventy Street in Sana'a? Have you participated in a protest against the treatment of the Akhdam, the destitute black people of Tihama in Yemen?"

Abdul-Raheem said, "These matters have nothing to do with Islam."

Saleh intervened, "But Prophet Muhammad (*may the greetings of Allah be upon him*) said that there was no difference between an Arab and a non-Arab except for the degree of piety. Muslims are also urged to want for their Muslim brethren the same as they would want for themselves."

Sam said, "The right of expression and freedom of speech have become universal, as well as the right to food, shelter, health and education. We're lucky in Lebanon, because we have reasonable rights notwithstanding the many different religious groups."

Samia countered, "I believe that you do so, *because* of the different ethnic and religious groups that make up Lebanon. That balance in numbers protects against having a majority group persecute a minority one. That balance is so important."

Sam added, "I also think that the Lebanese have had more than their fair share of civil war, and they've now learnt their lesson. But it won't take much to reignite animosities. Some people mock our sharing of the major political positions of president, prime minister and parliamentary leaders, but I think it's the most stable formula that's available to us – at least for now."

Saleh said, "We have to keep reminding ourselves that the only thing that does not change is change itself. Society will evolve with the changes in communications and technology and climate change. And we need to be innovative and above all open-minded, if we want peace and prosperity for all."

Abdul-Raheem said, "We all have read, that during the Abbasid dynasty, the Arabs were leaders in the fields of science, the arts and civilization in general, when Baghdad was the capital of all that. So, how can we blame Islam for our current woes?"

"For me, it's obvious," Saleh responded. "That was one united empire, admittedly a caliphate, but many of the caliphs were good at conducting the affairs of the state. First, that empire had not been invaded by the British, the French and the Italians, and parceled into numerous weak sheikhdoms, fighting each other as is the case now. Education is abysmal in the Arab world at present. We have some of the highest rates of illiteracy in the world, and those who can read, tend to read the Quran, which tells them things like 'O believers, obey Allah and his Prophet and those who are in charge of you.' which gives *carte blanche* to those dictatorial sheikhs and generals to do with their subjects what they want."

Abdul-Raheem snapped back, "With all due respect, Professor, you're selective in your quotations. Islam also told us '*Wa amruhom shoora bainahom*' which is all about consultation and democracy."

Saleh responded, "Yes, thanks for the correction. So, Muslims are getting mixed messages which leave us at the mercy of those in charge. In practice, this means being at the mercy of the children and grandchildren of those rulers until some military megalomaniac comes along and makes us obey him, at the point of a gun, usually made in the USA or Britain. And then the cycle continues when he passes us down to his own children."

Samia added, "That's exactly why we should never conflate the church, or in this case, the mosque, and the state.

That, above all, is the cause of the abysmal status of the Arabs."

Sam said, "I can tell you that the Christians I know feel the same way about democracy and the role of the church in their lives. They, too, are becoming increasingly secular."

Samia added, "But those religious and hereditary leaders will not voluntarily let go of their power. It'll take long-term education, exposure to democratic systems in the West, and it'll take a few martyrs too, and a lot of organization, in the face of vicious secret police networks, with paid informers, and a *carte blanche* for torture from the rulers."

"There are no easy answers," Saleh said. "All the campaigns for freedom and democracy in Europe, since the French Revolution, were bloody and difficult. But in the end, they achieved this separation of the state from the church, and the granting of rights to all citizens, irrespective of race, religion or gender. Once that occurs, people find it easier to live together in one country and work together in one industry. Take this country, the UK, for example. The English, Scots, Welsh and the Irish had many differences of origin, language and religion, and fought vicious wars against each other. But then they were able to form one country, where human rights are guaranteed for everyone, including the Polish or Indian immigrants, and the rule of law applies to the bus driver as much as the Minister of Defence."

Abdul-Raheem answered, "Having listened to you, Doctor, I must say that I have no hope of a united Arab nation. And the wise men and poets of the nation agree with me. And yet, here we are, four people, of different religions, from three different countries, meeting every week to share our worries, enjoying the company of each other, and sharing our thoughts so freely. So, there's something that links us together."

Saleh agreed, "Of course, there are things that link us, some good, some bad! But the main reason that we're able to meet every week, and want to continue, is that we're not in our countries. We're all either British citizens, or immigrants, with full rights and obligations in this democratic country. We know that we can talk like we've been doing without being arrested, and we can publish what we discuss on the internet, or stand on a soap box in Hyde Park and criticize the foreign minister, the Queen, or God Himself. If we had even a small part of this in Egypt, we would be thrilled. Because of that, back in our countries, we try to find protection by belonging to a group, either tribal or religious.

Sam said, "And that's what encourages the divide-and-rule system, which allows the dictator to neutralize one group, then another, then another, knowing that the Druze will not come to the rescue of the *Shiites*, and the Catholics will not help the *Sunnis*, because the *Sunnis* did not help them when they were victims, the year before."

Saleh agreed, "Absolutely! And this applies, not only to individuals, or sectarian groups, but also to whole countries, in other words different rulers."

"What do you mean?" Sam asked.

Saleh continued, "For example, in 1948, when the Egyptian army was fighting the Israeli army, in an attempt to establish a Palestinian state in Gaza, King Abdullah, the grandfather of the present king, instructed the British commander of the armed forces, General Glubb Pasha, not to help. Then, in 1967, the Egyptians sent misleading information to Syria and Jordan during the reign of King Hussein, which led to the participation of those two countries in a losing battle. All this to say that the so-called Arab League of over twenty countries is made up of dictatorships that, not only do not trust each other, but plot against each other."

Samia lamented, "What a contrast with, say, the European Union, where they don't even have a common language. They communicate very well through translation. Instead, they have democracy, and the rule of law."

Saleh asked, "Freedom House in London evaluates countries according to the level of democracy. Guess where the Arab countries lie on a scale of zero to ten?"

There were no takers.

Saleh continued, "As a group, they scored 3.6 out of 10, behind a country in Central Africa, like the Congo!"

Sam suggested, "These governments need to pay a lot of attention to the rule of law, instead of *Sharia* or any other form of religious laws."

Abdul-Raheem asked, "But which laws are you going to use?"

"There are already very well-established laws, such as English and French law, which can be modified to suit different countries," Sam replied, "But these can be modified by an act of parliament if necessary. I mean, at one point, when Lincoln was president, slavery was legal in the USA. But after the American Civil War, it was changed by congress. Had it been based on the Bible, this may not have happened. I just saw on the internet that African refugees are being sold in Libya as slaves for four hundred dollars each!"

Abdul-Raheem protested, "I find that we, in this group tend to go overboard in criticizing ourselves, and never remember that the West has its own set of faults."

"I don't agree with you there," Saleh countered. "We do criticize the West, and we are allowed if not encouraged to do so. But the greatest proof that the West is doing well is right here in this room."

"What do you mean?" Abdul-Raheem said, glancing round the room.

"The mere fact that we all have abandoned our countries of birth, that we four are here! We can talk freely. We can join a political party. We can readily find a lawyer to defend us, if we are accused of anything. And I have lived very happily in Germany, and visited Denmark, too. And you, Abdul-Raheem, moved your whole family here. They're not going back. And you will probably be buried here... long after I am!"

There was a long silence. You could have heard a pin drop.

Tina suddenly joined the discussion, "I know I'm young and green, but I've been listening to your very interesting conversation for nearly an hour. I'm really glad my friend Alex is late, because I've learnt a lot today."

"Thank you for saying that, Tina," Saleh said. "That's great. So what conclusions have you come to?"

"Well… the first thing I want to do is to thank my Mom for giving birth to me here, and not in Egypt!" Tina said. "And the second is that we young people simply don't realize how lucky we are, compared to young people in the Middle East. I mean, we're always complaining about this and about that, like money, transportation, the government, school fees, the papers and TV, the weather, and our teachers and even about our mothers!"

Sam said, "I can fully appreciate why you'd complain about *her*, Tina. I do, too."

Everyone laughed.

Samia said, "You never give up, Sam, do you?"

Saleh asked Tina, "And what would you say you've learned from this conversation?"

Tina replied, "Well, I've thought often enough about travelling to Egypt, you know, the land of my ancestors, basking in the sun, swimming in the Nile, and all that. But now I know how awful conditions over there are for young Egyptian students. I mean, if they can't even enjoy the basic necessities of life, like, health, food, shelter, who cares about the freedom to speak on a soap box in Hyde Park Corner?"

Samia, somewhat tearful, said, "Well said, my love! You make me and your *giddoo (great uncle)* very proud of you."

Saleh said, "I'll second that! Do you sometimes experience any strong identity problems here, Tina?"

"No, not at all," Tina replied. "Probably because I was born here, and Mom made sure that I felt and acted British. She did not teach me Arabic, except at the very beginning before Dad left us. So, I don't have any identity conflict, or divided loyalty."

Saleh asked, "But when you come across other Arab students, do they consider you one of them?"

Tina replied, "No, they don't, partly because I don't speak Arabic, and I 'pass' for a Brit of some kind. But if they ask, I tell them that my mother is Egyptian. They soon find out that

I don't have that Middle Eastern culture that they are used to, though."

Saleh continued, "So, do you feel left out?"

Tina replied, "Not at all. I don't feel Egyptian and I don't behave like one. I think I'm lucky that way because I don't feel conflicted. Why should I feel different to other Brits even if my mother is an immigrant?"

Alex arrived. By then Tina was more than ready to leave!

Saleh announced, "Perfect timing, Alex! On that note and brilliant answer, why don't we call it a day, and regroup in a couple of weeks, as usual?"

Chapter 14
Back at the Café Mocha

The weather was beautiful that day, and the café was crowded. But the group managed to find a table in the corner. Greetings being over, the discussion was re-started by Samia.

Samia said, "*A propos* our discussion two weeks ago, about the countries of the Middle East, I found out that there's an international organization called the Reputation Institute which evaluates countries according to their achievements in the fields of safety, education, economics, governance etc. It publishes an annual list of the top fifty-five countries."

Saleh agreed, "Yes, I remember that, in 2015, Canada was number one."

Samia continued, "So, guess where in that list some of the Arab countries ranked?"

There was silence.

Samia continued, "None of them were even on the list, and I'm sure they never will be, despite their enormous wealth."

Abdul-Raheem commented, "We don't have the necessary leaders to make us march forwards, like Gandhi or Mandela."

Saleh countered, "Actually, they're there! But you'll only find them in Arab jails, or in the West, in fear of persecution or prosecution by the military or hereditary dictators running their countries. Where would they have access to newspapers or TV or radio to reach their own citizens with their ideas? These are mostly privately owned or government owned, and they're busy spreading the info, I mean misinformation and propaganda for their governments or distracting their nations with music, beauty pageants, grand openings of shopping malls by dignitaries, and with rulers sending telegrams to each other on the occasion of the start of the holy month of *Ramadan*, and twenty-nine days later, at the end of the holy month. I mean, where is there time for anything else?"

Samia lamented, "I wish those *émigrés* who have the means would speak out a lot more!"

Saleh responded, "Some do. But they soon find themselves attacked, smeared, demonized and banned from travelling. I try to listen to people like Tariq Ramadan, who said something like 'The Arab Muslim world needs not only a political revolution, but also a revolution of thought, emanating from within, in order to change the economic systems, and to liberate education, art and religion, including the issue of gender equality'. And then he added something very crucial about Islam, when he said, 'Islam should be a tool for political innovation, rather than a hurdle to progress'. I hope I have repeated his statement correctly. So far, I've not heard of any assassination attempts against him."

"That's encouraging," Sam said.

Samia agreed, "I wish more Muslims would listen to that, and would teach it in their educational institutions. That stuff should be part of the Friday sermon, somewhere."

Saleh countered, "There's no way that would happen or be allowed. It's as though you were asking the dictator to organize his own demise. Which leader, even in democratic Europe would want that? What might be palatable is to promote the idea of separation of the state from the mosque, or the church, as the slogan goes in Europe. Otherwise, every time we try to modify something, we'll be frustrated by some text in Sharia, or by a specific interpretation of that text. And each time, the mullahs will win "

Samia said, "I hear you, uncle. They'll be repeating that mantra that *Sharia* is valid for every era and every location, and whoever tries to change that will be declared an apostate. We have a big problem. We're the masters of self-praise and of exaggeration... even in poetry, something I still love to read."

Abdul-Raheem objected, "That's not fair. The Latin nations, like the Italians and the Spaniards also tend to exaggerate. And the Scots... I'll bet you, you couldn't find a prouder nation."

Saleh resumed, "We've been talking about the abysmal status of the Arabs for weeks and going around and around in circles. We had so many accurate observations from everyone. I think that our diagnoses were fair and accurate. We considered possible remedies. But we have not put a finger on remedies that are likely to succeed. The remedies we suggested will be fought against tooth and nail by those in power in the state or in the 'church', in this case, the 'mosque'. Is it time to repeat the famous saying of the Egyptian statesman, Saad Zaghloul, who turned to his wife, and said, 'It's no use!' What do the younger people think?"

Samia said, "I guess I can understand why the older generation wants to give up, when they see no hope. But the younger generation can't afford to do that, because they can't accept the status quo for the next half century. So, it's up to us to persuade our friends and colleagues and anyone prepared to listen that we have to turn a new leaf."

Saleh agreed, "That's very good to hear. So, what should we do?"

Samia replied, "We should stop talking about the glorious past, and make everyone understand that the past was great, but will not come back. We should stop bragging about Omar Ibn Al-Khattab, and Khaled Ibn Alwaleed and Tariq bin Ziyad. They belong to a completely different era. Obviously, there are no female names of note, which is typical of our culture. Let's turn a completely new page and see how we can improve the future for us, and more importantly, for our children, like Tina here. We must urge everyone to have a frank and honest debate about where we go from here. Those who start to call us names especially apostates, should be debated, and if that fails, should be ignored and marginalized. Slowly but surely, logic and science and freedom of thought and of speech will take over. We *have* to be prepared for disappointments and setbacks, because the extremist will *not* leave us alone. But, slowly, change will occur. It has to! We also need to honour those who have taken that progressive path before us, like Bourguiba in Tunisia."

Saleh said, "People will tell you that you cannot pick and choose from *Sharia* what you like. They use that tactic often. Make sure you answer them with 'says who?'. Of course, you can pick and choose those parts that suit you. You can choose to fast during *Ramadan*, while banning polygamy and female genital mutilation. You can make the value of a woman's evidence in court the same as that of a man. Tunisia has just permitted a Muslim woman to marry a non-Muslim man, and the country is still standing tall."

Abdul-Raheem protested, "I don't agree with any of that. I think that tinkering with *Sharia*, which comes from God, is wrong. He created those laws, in His wisdom, which cannot be doubted."

Samia countered, "You have the right to think that and to say that, and you can use God as your excuse to maintain the status quo. But permit me the right to propose changes, and let us debate our opposing positions in public, without fear of assassination, and may the best man – or woman in this case – win. That's what needs to happen."

Sam teased, "I'll vote for the woman anytime! I agree. There's no other way today in the twenty-first century. And I am also including Christianity, not only Islam, when I say this. I read Ayan Hirsi's controversial book soon after it was published. She advocated several actions; that the Quran should not be interpreted literally, that *Sharia* should be updated to be compatible with modern times, the list of what is taboo should be modified, armed jihad should be stopped, and our focus should be on success in life instead of in the hereafter."

Samia concurred, "Yes, I read it, too. I also read Salman Rushdi's book for which he received a very serious death threat. He was saying that Muslims should consider the emergence of Islam as an important historical event, and the Quran as a historical document which can be interpreted in a manner consistent with the period of time in which we live.

That way, *Sharia*, written in the seventh century, could be updated to be compatible with modern times."

Abdul-Raheem said, "I think those two went too far, and therefore caused so much friction and anger. On the other hand, Professor Tariq Ramadan whom we mentioned earlier, a Swiss citizen, originally from your country, Samia, said, what was a lot more acceptable to me – and people like me. He said that the Arab-Muslim world is in need, not only of a political revolution, but also of an intellectual one in order to modify the current economic system, and to liberate our understanding of art, culture and religion, including that of gender equality. That should make you happy, Samia."

Samia shook her head.

Sam said, "I was saddened to see that the Christian Mayor of the capital of Indonesia was jailed for a statement he made that angered the Muslim majority. He had heard that some Muslim groups were urging the citizens not to vote for him, since that would make a non-Muslim their boss, and they used some verse from the Quran to make the point. So, it was natural that he would refer to that verse, and give an alternative interpretation of it, namely that it was not sinful for a Muslim to vote for a non-Muslim."

Saleh said, "I feel frustrated by stories of that kind. I mean, my own mother tongue is Arabic, and yet I have great difficulty interpreting the Quran. It's not easy to sort out the meaning or intention of some phrases. It wouldn't surprise me if someone lost their life in those riots, but I didn't check. It gives Muslims a bad name, that's all. As if they needed any more bad press!"

Samia concurred, "The thing is, we don't know for absolutely sure that these words are those of Allah."

Abdul-Raheem snapped back angrily, "Of course, they are! Of course! How can you say that? But I accept that there may be slight differences in the interpretation."

Samia said, "OK. I am happy to concede that. We have just spent a few weeks discussing the very thorny issue of Islam, and we decided to listen to each other, without labelling each other as *kafir* or apostate. This is not the Middle East.

This is London, the capital of free speech for the past one hundred years. If you are so sure it is the word of God, because I am *not*, then answer me this: Why was the Quran sent to us by Allah, in Arabic?"

Abdul-Raheem said without hesitation, "Because it was revealed to Prophet Muhammad (peace be upon him). It couldn't have been sent to him in English!"

Samia countered, "Obviously. But Islam is supposed to be a message to all the people of this world, not just those who speak or understand Arabic."

Abdul-Raheem replied, "And we should be very happy and grateful to have been chosen to receive that message."

Samia asked, "So, are you saying that we too are chosen?"

Abdul-Raheem said, "Chosen to spread the word of Allah to other nations."

Samia asked, "So, the Arabs, or their prophet, are supposed to spread it to the billion Chinese, and the billion Indians, and the billion South Americans? Isn't that a very inefficient way of spreading a message?"

Abdul-Raheem snapped back, "Look, Samia I don't question the actions of Allah, or his wisdom. It had to be sent to *someone*!"

"I just think along simple logical lines," Samia replied. "If I wanted a message to reach six billion people, I'd send it to the group that had the largest population and urge them to tell the others. Or, if I had infinite resources, I'd send it to all of them at the same time. Wouldn't you?"

Abdul-Raheem said, "We are talking here about God, not a manager of an email company. He has infinite wisdom, and no one has the right to doubt his wisdom."

Samia responded, "Look! I know that you're a devout believer, and I don't want to hurt your feelings. I really do wish that the Quran, which is a wonderful book with so much wisdom, and a lot of history, had been sent out in Chinese, or possibly English. Because if it had spread rapidly from China to most of the world, most people would probably have converted to Islam by now, and so many religious wars would have been avoided, and millions of people would not have been killed. You would like that, wouldn't you?"

Abdul-Raheem answered, "Of course, but I'd never ever appoint myself judge over the actions of the Almighty. He, alone, judges. Our role is to obey without question. He says in the Quran, 'I know what you do not know'."

Sam joined in, "I don't really want to insert myself into a debate between two Muslims, but I need to add that this complete submission to God without questioning is not peculiar to Islam. We have the same attitude in the Christian church, in all its subdivisions, and I suspect that the other major religions are in the same boat."

Abdul-Raheem agreed, "Yes, of course, and as we all know, the Quran is full of stories about Moses and Jesus and Mary, and Abraham, and Joseph and Isaac, etc."

Samia persisted, "All religions, as I see it, are concerned with two things; our behaviour on this earth, and our fate after death. The first part is easy. I think there is universal agreement that if we are pious and kind and caring and good to our fellow women and men, we feel good about it, and believe that we will be rewarded after death. Personally, I would subscribe to this fully, because I happen to think that I have fulfilled my vows and promises to myself. The second part of this is not clear to me. I have to admit that I find it extremely difficult to imagine the second part. If I cannot even imagine it, how can I possibly subscribe to it?"

Abdul-Raheem opined, "This is the real difference between the believer and the non-believer. The former believes the word of God and has no doubts. He prays a lot and sleeps soundly. The doubter is troubled."

Samia agreed, "I happen to agree with you. My father used to say to me, 'For those who believe, no proof is necessary, and for those who don't no proof is possible.' He was a believer, of course. But what if you are wrong?"

Abdul-Raheem responded, "I can ask *you* the same question. But even if I am wrong, I will have still lived a pious life, praying and meditating and doing good in the world."

Samia said, "If I am wrong, I'm in trouble! I'll be punished for not believing and presumably not rewarded for my good deeds, because I was not a believer. But I will be with the majority of people."

Saleh intervened, "At this important conclusion, I suggest that we adjourn till next week."

Chapter 15
Right and Wrong

At the subsequent meeting, Samia was prepared with a question which she always wanted to ask, but never had the opportunity to do.

Samia started, "Please allow me to ask a question about something that has bothered me for a long time. And once again about the Quran, although I do so reluctantly, in case, it annoys someone."

The three men nodded their heads, looking puzzled.

Samia said, "I keep asking myself what would happen to all those billions of people who lived and died before any of these religions appeared."

Abdul-Raheem was quick to respond, "They did not commit any sin, because they lived well before these different religions arrived."

Samia said, "Makes sense, but how do you know that?"

Abdul-Raheem answered, "It is logical, because they lived before Islam."

Samia reiterated, "You're saying that the message of Islam never reached them?"

Abdul-Raheem confirmed, "Exactly."

Samia continued, "But there were several older religions. So, do they go to paradise or to hell?"

Abdul-Raheem hesitated, then muttered, "I... I... I don't know."

Samia persisted, "But my understanding is that on the day of reckoning, they, and all other animals and plants and insects and bacteria, on earth and on any other planets, will be processed and judged by God. Isn't this what we learnt as Muslims when we were kids?"

Sam joined with, "And as Christians too."

Samia resumed, "And presumably, the Hindus, whom we keep ignoring in all our discussions even though there are one billion of them, and even though they are changing this world with their spectacular scientific achievements? You know, they have become experts in nuclear bombs, ballistic missiles and much more, and occupy very sensitive positions all over the world. Even the Chinese are watching them carefully."

Sam agreed, "Indeed! They follow a very well-established religion and subscribe to the importance of doing good as opposed to being evil. We never talk about them or their beliefs or their achievements or their contributions to civilization. And they have subdivisions, such as Sikhism, which apparently espouses some of the principles of Islam. Are they mentioned at all in the Quran, or the pronouncements of Prophet Muhammad?"

Abdul-Raheem replied, "I don't believe so."

Samia continued, "That's what's puzzling me! Why did the Quran not mention them but talks about 'the people of the book', referring to the three youngest religions; which proves that one's religion depends very heavily on one's place of birth, first and foremost. Or is it, perhaps, because these are the three youngest religions."

Abdul-Raheem said, "The three religions we've been discussing share a history of the Middle East, as opposed to the Indian subcontinent or China? Needless to say, if all those Indians and Chinese millions were born in the Arabian Peninsula, they would have grown up Muslim or Christian or Jewish. That's my understanding of the situation."

Samia said, "We know that they were not born in the Middle East. But the question is why are they never included in the discussion. Stats show that the largest religious group is the Christian one with just over two billion, followed by the Muslims with just over one and a half billion, followed by the Hindus with one billion, then the Buddhists with four hundred thousand, followed by the Sikhs, who are estimated to be thirty million. Finally, the Jews, who often make the news, are about fourteen million, less than the population of Cairo. The good news, for me, is that those who have no religious affiliation are a whole billion, and are increasing steadily, at the expense of the major religions."

Abdul-Raheem responded, "Is this solid verifiable data, Samia, or is it your wishful thinking?"

Samia admitted, "Both, actually! But this raises a question, which I hope you all will hear, without calling me apostate."

Abdul-Raheem said, "Please go ahead. I won't. I'm quite impressed with your research into all this."

Samia replied, "Thank you. Likewise! What I am wondering is whether the reason why Judaism and Christianity are frequently mentioned in the Quran is that Muhammad used to travel from Mecca to Syria, in a caravan laden with goods, for sale or exchange with goods from Syria. There he rubbed shoulders with Jews and Christians, and when he returned to Mecca to give the profits to his employer Khadija, he talked to her about his adventures there. Later, he married her, of course."

Abdul-Raheem agreed, "That's certainly documented."

Samia continued, "So, is it remotely conceivable – and once again I am saying it is only a hypothesis – that Muhammad enunciated the Quran based on his experiences in Syria? And that is why there are no tales about Alexander of Macedonia or the Moguls in India or the tribes of Africa?"

Abdul-Raheem, with obvious exasperation said, "No, no, no! The Quran is the word of God, not Muhammad. There is *no* room for doubt or discussion on this issue. But because Muhammad was illiterate, he had to recite the verses to a literate man named Waraqa bin Nofal, and he wrote them down."

Saleh began somberly, "I'm going to speak my mind. I'm not afraid of being attacked as an apostate. I admit that, like everyone else, I have no monopoly on the truth, and indeed I don't even know the truth. But… but what I've heard now and previously tells me that the text of the Quran was provided by

Muhammad; yes, by Muhammad, because I just cannot accept that Allah would announce it or recite it in Arabic, and leave out all the hundreds of other languages of this world, and will expect from their scholars to translate it, given how complex it is, but also how crucial its instructions are for the smooth function and order of society. You all know how much debate can occur over one phrase or one word of the Quran, even among people whose mother tongue is Arabic."

Abdul-Raheem shouted, "No, no, no! I cannot and will not listen to such talk!"

Silence reigned over the group for a whole minute.

Samia asked, "Abdul-Raheem! Do you believe that all people will be judged after death?"

"Yes, of course!" Abdul-Raheem said. "The Quran says, whoever performs a grain of good, or a grain of evil, will be rewarded or punished accordingly."

Saleh interjected, "I enjoyed reading an article which discussed why most people are convinced that there is this absolute power, which we call 'God'. It seems that eighty percent of people are believers, although the God they believe in is different for each group. Apparently, there are hundreds of subcategories of the religions we hear about, maybe even thousands. This article puts forward the concept that people believe in two powers or forces; during life, there is the government which determines punishments for crimes, but there is a divine force which punishes people who somehow escape punishment by their government."

Sam joined the conversation, "That makes sense to me, because the lower, poorer classes, who suffer so many injustices during life, would indeed want there to be such a divine force that will avenge those injustices which escaped punishment during life."

Saleh added, "It could also be due to their lack of opportunity to acquire education, which would have allowed them to ponder these matters in greater depth."

"Yes, that's a good point," Sam said. "I didn't consider that. For example, my little sister died in her infancy, whereas my brother and I reached this age. So, why was she so unlucky? What has she done to deserve that?"

"This is fate, as determined by God. We accept it without protest and without question," Abdul-Raheem answered.

Sam responded, "Yes, I know. In any case, protest does not bring back the dead."

Abdul-Raheem asked, "Was she ill?"

Sam said, "Yes. She was premature, delivered at seven months, so she was retarded and spastic, and hardly could talk."

Abdul-Raheem said, "The cause is obvious in this case."

Sam persisted, "Of course, that contributed to the problem. But the question is why was she born like that in the first place? What had she done to deserve that fate?

Abdul-Raheem answered, "We Muslims say that it's all in the hands of Allah."

Sam persisted again, "And I am asking what has she done to deserve that horrible fate? Was God testing her patience and tolerance and faith while she was only a few days old, and then died at two years?"

Abdul-Raheem said, "We cannot question the wisdom of Allah."

Sam said, "I knew you'd say that, even though we always call Allah the Merciful several times a day. My question, which you will no doubt find provocative and rude, is: Where is His mercy?"

Abdul-Raheem, taken aback, asked, "OK. How would *you* explain it then?"

Sam replied, "Christians also have the same lack of answer. Me personally, I see nothing but injustice here. But let's ask Doctor Saleh."

Saleh intervened, "The old debate about whether man's actions are his own or are directed by God still rages on. The scientific explanation is easy. She was born well before her brain growth and blood circulation were complete which meant that the supply of oxygen to her brain was deficient. This made her limbs spastic which in turn limited her breathing, and resulted in inflammations in the lungs, which most people know as pneumonia. But there are other horrendous things that happen to the fetus during pregnancy, which I can tell you about if you're interested."

Sam blurted, "Sure."

Saleh resumed, "You probably read about a drug called thalidomide, which was used to calm pregnant women. This caused the lack of growth of the limbs in the fetus which meant that some children were born with short arms or legs, so short that they couldn't feed themselves, or even go to the bathroom by themselves."

Sam said, "That's horrible. What I read was that all these drugs that are invented or developed are always tested on animals, then on human volunteers before being launched."

Saleh continued, "You're correct. But pregnant women are usually excluded from such trials. So, the new drug was not tested during pregnancy. So, who is responsible for the suffering of these babies?"

Abdul-Raheem said, "The scientists who did not test the drug extensively enough."

Saleh said, "I agree, but it was unintended, and the drug trial was done according to the written regulations, in other words women were not tested. But after the medication was approved for the market, when pregnant women used it, it affected the fetus in the early stages of limb development. But the problem I have is that the *mullahs* keep telling us that everything that happens to man, woman or child, or animal, or plant is from fate controlled by Allah. So, do you agree with that?"

Abdul-Raheem replied, "God is always merciful, but we also know that man will fall sick and will suffer and will die. The Quran says in the chapter of *Al Imran,* 'Every soul shall experience death, then will return to us'."

Saleh said, "Well, of course, every living thing will eventually die, from the elephant to the ant. But the question is what role does God play in all that? If it's all under his command, then how can he allow such suffering to a new-born baby?"

Abdul-Raheem stated, "Muslims believe that Allah is testing their faith, and that the real faithful ones never lose it."

Saleh conceded, "I'll go along with you there, but surely not when that person is a baby who cannot think or talk, but dies at the age of a few days or hours."

Samia intervened, "I think we've flogged this issue to death. Can we please change the subject? Does anyone know how many humans, on this earth, die every day?"

Abdul-Raheem said, "No idea, but it must be in the many thousands."

Samia continued, "There are complete stats on all such questions, thanks to the internet. The estimate is fifty million a year. It's like if the whole population of Spain dies that year. And can you guess the age of our world?"

Abdul-Raheem said, "I have no idea either. Fifty thousand? It's just a wild guess."

Samia said, "Look! Jesus goes back two thousand years, right? But based on scientific research, man as we know him today, walking upright on two legs, started to live on this earth four hundred thousand years ago – at a minimum. But let's be conservative in our estimates. That period of time is like the two centuries since Christ multiplied by two hundred. But that is the minimum. Some Canadian archaeologist or scientist unearthed the fossilized bones of a unicorn which are estimated to be more than a million years. A million years! Its weight was estimated to be three thousand pounds, which would equal that of twenty average men. But it is reported to have two horns, not one."

Abdul-Raheem said, "But these are numbers that defy our imagination."

Samia stated, "Of course, but these figures also suggest that since Christ was around, the number of human deaths might be fifty million persons, times two thousand years, which equals one hundred thousand million. That's one hundred billion. And, if we now extend this farther back, to the beginning of the two-legged man, supposedly four hundred thousand years, we can assume that the number of dead humans may reach twenty thousand billion, which is twenty *trillion* dead people!"

Abdul-Raheem said, "It is difficult to imagine such numbers."

Samia answered, "I can't imagine such numbers either. What I do to even begin to imagine these astronomical figures is to imagine how many earths they would occupy of they all suddenly reappeared on the same day. So, if we divide twenty thousand billion people by seven billion, which is the current population of this earth, the answer would be 20,000 divided by seven, which is approximately 3000 earths, needed to accommodate them… assuming they are buried, not cremated!"

Saleh and Sam began to laugh, Abdul-Raheem continued to look puzzled.

Abdul-Raheem protested, "This can't be right. These numbers are just too huge to comprehend. There must be a mistake in your calculation, Samia, with all due respect. I know you're used to looking at figures of millions at your bank, but I just can't follow this. Anyway, this theory of Darwin is only a theory. How can a monkey possibly become a human being?"

Saleh explained, "I must say I sympathize with you Abdul-Raheem. These are such huge figures, that are difficult to imagine, but they do make sense, and I did check the calculations. They *are* correct, if we assume that the number of annual deaths in the whole world is close to that of the population of Spain, around fifty million. But I'll add something about evolution, since my scientific background allows me to do that.

Evolution is a real thing. I'll quickly give you a real-life example. There is a type of lizard which inhabits the forest, and has long limbs, which permit it to quickly climb the branches of a tree. But the same species of that lizard, which lives in the desert, or flat ground, has distinctly shorter legs. So, some smart scientists performed an experiment, and transferred some forest lizards to the desert. Over several generations, which took about ten years, they found that those long-legged lizards developed progressively shorter legs! So, what do you think of that?"

Abdul-Raheem replied, "You scientists do strange things. I don't know whether to believe that or not. But I do believe whatever the Quran says, and whatever the Prophet (peace be upon him) said."

Saleh said, "Samia, there's a minor correction to your calculation. You assumed that the number of deaths in the world is around fifty million, similar to the population of Spain or here in the UK. But that world population has *not* always been the fifty billion of today. It was much lower, thousands of years ago. However, the formula is still correct in principle, and even if we assume that the number of the dead is only ten percent of the Spanish population, the numbers are still mind boggling! And we will still need three hundred, not three thousand, earths to accommodate them."

Samia said, "Thanks, Uncle. Good point."

Abdul-Raheem protested, "But how did those scientists arrive at such figures about the age of those graves?"

Saleh said, "This has recently become possible because of the new science of carbon dating. One can determine the age of carbon molecules in bones and other tissues. But another relevant question would be, if and when the day of resurrection arrives, would all those dead people be at the ages and states of health at the time of their death? Will the eighty-year-old paraplegic woman who died in her wheelchair come back in that same state of health? At the same age of eighty? And will she live forever in that state? And the spastic baby of three months, will he be allowed to grow into an adult? Never mind all the billions of animals and insects and viruses, etc.?"

Abdul-Raheem sighed and said, "Only Allah knows."

Samia asked, "And what about a baby from a Muslim family in Nigeria who was eaten by a crocodile, who in turn was eaten by a tiger, what happens to him, and to the tiger and crocodile? And would his fate be any different if he belonged to a Buddhist family in Myanmar?"

Saleh joined in, "That's a great question. Obviously, no one is going to volunteer an answer, but let me share something I learnt during my scientific career. It's about viruses. Several years ago, on an island called Papua New Guinea, a female scientist noticed that women, but not men, were dying because of a fatal illness which destroyed their brains. After a lot of study, she came to the conclusion that it was because the population practiced cannibalism. But she asked the crucial question: Why only the women? I suppose, if I put that question to an *Imam*, he would, without hesitation, tell me that it was the will of Allah. But this scientist found out that when a family member died, the men, who are nearly always considered better than the women, in most cultures, would eat the dead person's flesh, as a sign of respect for that dead man, believe it or not! And when the men have finished eating the meat, the rest of the body was left for the women to feed on. That included the brain. She studied those brains and found out that they contained microscopic cysts cause by a slow infectious virus, which would go into the bloodstream of those women, and from there to their brains, and they in turn would die."

Abdul-Raheem exclaimed, "How disgusting! Go on! I noticed something important in this story."

Saleh asked, "Yes? What was it?"

Abdul-Raheem replied, "Everyone keeps blaming Muslims for treating their women as second-class citizens. What could be worse than this example that you described to us?"

Saleh agreed, "Absolutely!"

Abdul-Raheem asked, "But if all the women died, how did the tribe manage to continue to multiply?"

Saleh replied, "An astute observation, my friend. Well, that tribe came close to extinction, until this custom was abolished. But now, my obvious question is: On the day of resurrection, according to Islam, what will happen to those people who were eaten? Will they reappear again? And the people who ate them, what happens to them? Which is similar to the question I asked about the child eaten by the crocodile."

Abdul-Raheem pondered, then said, "A very difficult question for me to answer, Doctor. We Muslims believe the verse in the *Surah* of *Naba'*, which says 'on the day, the bugle is sounded, you will come in waves...' But all those statistics which Samia was calculating, I am not convinced by them. There must be some error there."

Samia responded, "You can do your own arithmetic. But I need to know what the fate of all those people will be. People born in their billions who died in their billions before any religions burst onto this world – never mind Islam. At least what happened to those innocent children who starved to death in your country of Yemen, or died like flies from cholera and diphtheria?"

Abdul-Raheem answered, "I cannot answer such questions, Samia. But I'm content to know that Allah is capable of everything, and we should all remember that."

Saleh remarked, "Those numbers are scary, and difficult to imagine, because whenever we talk about religions, we think about Moses crossing the desert, and Jesus on the crucifix and Muhammad in his cave, or on his way to Medina, being welcomed by its singing residents. But, to help myself imagine that length of time I resort to diagrams. And, if you like, I will share with you the one I am using."

Everyone shook their heads in agreement.

Saleh continued, "I would like you, one day, to buy some match boxes, and line up the contents of about twenty such boxes, end to end along your living room floor. You'll need four hundred match sticks. If each matchstick is five centimeters, that's two inches if you prefer inches, then lining up the two hundred sticks would make a straight line of twenty meters or sixty-six feet. Take matchsticks numbers three hundred and ninety-nine, and four hundred and color them red or blue, whatever you like.

Sam looked puzzled and said, "This all sounds very intriguing!"

Saleh continued, "We're almost there. I myself, only understood all this after I lined up the match sticks. Now, I would like you to imagine that each red matchstick represents one thousand years. The period of time since Jesus died, which is two thousand years, is represented by the two red sticks. The next three matchsticks cover the period when Buddhism and Judaism appeared. Thus, the head of the red matchstick would represent now, us, here, in this room, having coffee. Now, I want you to follow that line with your eyes to the last match stick, which as I explained, was the point in the age of the universe four hundred thousand years ago. Man is supposed to have started his life journey around Lake Victoria in Africa and spread from there. I know that there is a lot of controversy about the origin of man and about the theory of evolution. But, as I explained before, there's also evidence that man goes back much longer than even that, perhaps a million years or even two million. Are you with me so far, Abdul-Raheem?"

Abdul-Raheem said, "Yes. Sounds fascinating! But what if all these numbers are wrong? What is the evidence?"

Saleh continued, "We Muslims and Christians tend to selfishly ignore Hinduism and Judaism and Buddhism and Sikhism, and the religions of the indigenous people of Canada, America and Australia. But if you read the literature, you will find some fascinating and convincing scientific data. One book that I've read is titled People of the Earth, by Brian Fagan, I think from the University of California. He showed that Homo erectus, that is man standing erect on his two legs, unlike his four-legged ancestors, the monkeys, dates back at least four hundred thousand years if not a million years or even two million!"

Abdul-Raheem observed, "So, all current religions are very recent in the life of the universe?"

Saleh confirmed, "That's the whole point of this exercise. The question now is: What will happen to all those people who died during that extremely long period represented by those three hundred and ninety-five match sticks? They never had the opportunity to follow Moses or Buddha or Jesus or Muhammad. Will they burn in hell? How can a just God allow that, if He, Himself, created all those women and children and men?"

Samia asked, "Maybe there's is no judgment day, after all?"

Sam suggested, "It's really scary. I find myself, a Christian born among a Muslim majority, wondering why and how my end should be any different from yours."

Samia said, "I've always wanted to ask this question, Sam. In Christianity, I understand that Jesus died on the cross in order that the sins of Christians would be forgiven. Is that true? And if so, why did Jesus have to go through that horrendous death? Why did your God not forgive Christians without the need for that crucifixion?"

Sam replied, "Good question, except to say that I have found throughout my life that everything surrounding religion is never straight forward or simple. That's why there's been so much conflict. It seems that all religions expect of us to believe but never question. That was fine, hundreds of years ago. But now with all this science, and the internet and the pace of life, it is very difficult not to challenge dogma. I've always asked myself, because I was afraid to ask others, how did a union between Adam and Eve could have produced all these different people with so many genetic differences, of shape and size, and colour of skin, and hair and eyes, and all these thousands of languages. And while we can imagine people migrating from Africa to Europe, how did man cross the Atlantic to the Americas? Perhaps our scientist friend can tell us?"

Saleh responded, "Like the rest of you, I don't know the truth about this life, and even less about hell and paradise. What we do know is that death is as certain as birth. We see it and we cause it, at times. We humans kill an ant or a wasp or shoot a poor sparrow with an air gun. Some show more courage, or perhaps more correctly, cruelty, and slit the throat of a goat to cook for the celebrations after *Ramadan*, and somehow dispose of its bones. In all these cases, although we can't document it in some animals, blood is spilled, resulting in depriving the brain-stem of its function. That brain stem is what controls our breathing as well as basic neurological reflexes, like blood pressure and body temperature. So, death

is a process, rather than a split-second event. In rare cases, if you can provide help that interrupts this process, life can return, or seem to return. This happens very successfully with hypothermia, such as drowning in a frozen lake."

Abdul-Raheem said, "God can show us miracles."

Saleh responded, "There is more than one way of interpreting these rare successes."

Samia joined in, "I kind of like the oriental concept that those who have been good in their lives return to life, after death, in the shape of a horse or an eagle, or some other noble animal, whereas bad or criminal people might come back as a cockroach, or a snake."

Saleh said, "As someone who is close to death, at least closer to death than you three younger people, I'd love that hypothesis to be true, but all my scientific training and logical thinking tells me otherwise."

Abdul-Raheem said, "I know that you don't share my opinion or beliefs, but I've really enjoyed debating it with all three of you, and I'm convinced that the word of Allah is supreme, and that He will reward me for my good deeds and will also punish me for my few sins."

Sam concluded, "I suspect that you three Muslims, albeit to different degrees, might think that you will go to paradise, where rivers will flow under your feet, and you will be eternally served by beautiful maidens and handsome young men, while I languish in hell forever. Well, I've got news for you, my friends. I'm coming to paradise too, by invitation or without it!"

All four burst into laughter.